IRMA and JERRY

Other Avon Camelot Books by
George Selden

OSCAR LOBSTER'S FAIR EXCHANGE
TUCKER'S COUNTRYSIDE

GEORGE SELDEN is the author of several acclaimed books for children, the most celebrated being the famous Cricket series: THE CRICKET IN TIMES SQUARE, TUCKER'S COUNTRYSIDE, HARRY CAT'S PET PUPPY, and CHESTER CRICKET'S PIGEON RIDE. He has also written a modern Arabian Nights tale, THE GENIE OF SUTTON PLACE, and a book about creatures who dwell in the sea, OSCAR LOBSTER'S FAIR EXCHANGE.

It is essential to Mr. Selden that his animal characters display the true emotions and feelings with which readers can identify. According to Mr. Selden, "A specific human characteristic, such as acquisitiveness, can be shown in sharpened, often comical exaggeration. However fantastic the adventures may be, the human truth that the animal characters embody must be clear, real, and accurate. What really makes a children's classic is exactly the same thing that makes an adult classic — good writing, sharp observation, and interesting incident with perhaps an extra pinch of belief. That is why a children's classic is a classic for everyone."

Mr. Selden was born in Hartford, Connecticut, and received his Bachelor of Arts from Yale University. He lives in New York City and enjoys music, archaeology, and J.R.R. Tolkien.

IRMA and JERRY
George Selden

Illustrated by Leslie H. Morrill

AN AVON CAMELOT BOOK

IRMA AND JERRY is an original publication of Avon Books. This work has never before appeared in book form.

6th grade reading level has been determined by using the Fry Readability Scale.

AVON BOOKS
A division of
The Hearst Corporation
959 Eighth Avenue
New York, New York 10019

Copyright © 1982 by George Selden Thompson
Cover and text illustrations Copyright © 1982 by Leslie H. Morrill
Book design by Sheldon Winicour
Published by arrangement with the author
Library of Congress Catalog Card Number: 82-6678
ISBN: 0-380-80978-8

Library of Congress Cataloging in Publication Data

Selden, George.
  Irma and Jerry.

  (An Avon Camelot book)
  Summary: The adventures of a cat and a dog living in New York City's Greenwich Village.
  [1. Cats—Fiction.   2. Dogs—Fiction.   3. New York (N.Y.)—Fiction.] I. Morrill, Leslie, H., ill. II. Title.
PZ7.T37154Ir   [Fic]   82-6678
ISBN 0-380-80978-8   AACR2

First Camelot Printing, October, 1982

CAMELOT TRADEMARK REG. U.S. PAT. OFF. AND IN OTHER COUNTRIES, MARCA REGISTRADA, HECHO EN U.S.A.

Printed in the U.S.A.

DON 10 9 8 7 6 5 4 3 2 1

To Edward J. Czerwinksi, once again,
who guards, with love, the seat of insight
between two trees

CONTENTS

IRMA AND JERRY

ONE

We Meet

I'm Jerry; Irma's a cat.

But dog though I am—a cocker spaniel, in fact, with a very attractive brown and white coat—I have to admit I was crying the first time that I met Irma. Yours truly was lost!

I and my family—the Thompsons, that is—had just moved to New York. We came down from New Haven, Connecticut, where my master and/or owner—and I may say my friend— Professor George Thompson gave up a position in the philosophy department at Yale, the university there, to teach the same subject at the New School for Social Research, in Greenwich Village, which is part of New York. The professor and I, I might add, have always had an excellent relationship— ever since I was a pup. He even takes me to class sometimes!

I overheard him and the missis talking one night, and the money was better, he said, in New York. But my private guess is, he was won over by the title they gave him down here: Distinguished Lecturer in Contemporary Philosophy. I could have been won by a title like that myself! (At least that's what Irma says.)

So down we three came to New York. A van took all the furniture, and the Thompsons and I—and a few other highly prized possessions—rode in the Thompsons' Volkswagen.

(The professor had hopes for a larger car when the new salary started coming in.)

They had rented a very nice duplex apartment on Charles Street, in Greenwich Village. The house was much older than our house in New Haven, and at first it made me feel queasy to think of all the dogs and people who had lived there before us. And also, since it was a town house converted into three apartments, there were two other tenants: a lawyer who had big thick glasses and always carried a bulging briefcase, and a single lady who worked at Macy's department store. I wasn't sure I liked sharing a house, but in New York you learn to like some things you never would have liked elsewhere. And also we didn't see much of the legal man or the Macy's lady. Most fortunately, they almost never came down to the basement.

Our house had a little rear garden too. I like to believe, although no one ever said so in words, that they took that apartment because of me. I was used to a yard in New Haven, and a garden, however cramped and small, is as near to a yard as you get in New York. Our particular garden has several rosebushes—my favorites—a plot for flowers, and a single well-placed tree in a corner, with a nice little private hedge around it.

My greatest and first mistake, that first day in New York—and it was the first of many, I am forced to admit—was to go exploring. The professor and the missis were telling the moving men where to position all the furniture, and I decided to venture forth. Now in New Haven—in *all* safe neighborhoods, I would assume—a dog goes exploring as a matter of course. But not in New York. In New York a dog who goes exploring gets lost. At least I did. However, in my own defense, I must say I've rather prided myself on my sense of direction. At least until then. It got mislaid somewhere around Bridgeport, I guess.

So many buildings! And most of them old. But they weren't quaint. I hate "quaint"! They were agéd and honorable—like a few human beings: mature and understanding and wise. And so many streets, with corners that all looked alike! I missed roads that curved; but that's New York. Very reasonably, it seemed to me, I took my bearings on three or four distin-guished old houses. A tulip tree stood in front of one of them. And I assumed I would find my way home. But alas, I could not. Distinguished the old New York houses may be—lined up like veterans from a long-ago war—but to a dog who's just come from New Haven, a lot of them look exactly the same. I was lost.

Although full-grown—not *old*, understand, or middle-aged yet—yours truly began to whimper a bit. First I got nervous—that isn't too unusual—and then panic set in. It embarrasses me dreadfully to admit this, of course, but—well, Irma says that sooner or later everyone gets reduced to the truth.

And the truth is, I was scared to death! Cars were roaring by—and even on the side streets too—the humans all were hurrying, including the ones who looked as if they had no place to go. The city's noises came suddenly close: I was absolutely petrified!

That's when I started to cry, I guess. (Oh dear—this is dreadful to confess! I was even on the verge of a howl.) I crept into a doorway, shivering, and my worst fear was gorging inside my throat when a voice said, "Whatsa matter, honey?"

A cat, of mixed parentage—Persian, Siamese, and some-thing that Irma called "just me"—had stopped by the doorway and was staring into the gloom where I crouched with a kind of mixed pity and quizzical curiosity. I could see that her fur was longish and more like amber than like the honey of your basic Siamese.

She made a cat sound—"Mmmmn!"—and then asked, "Are you lost?"

I must tell you now about Irma's purr. And how shall I describe it, lacking Shakespeare's gift for words? (Which later I did acquire.) It wasn't "Rrrrr," like your ordinary cat's comment. It was more like a philosophical "Hummmm"—as if her silent thinking and musing came out in a wise, under-standing sound. The depths of its feline intuition sent chills down my back even then.

I licked my chops—which is something we dogs often do, to clear our minds as well as our mouths. I *was* lost, of course, but lost or not, I could hardly forget that I still was a dog, with a dog's obligations. I bared my teeth, as best I could, and made the classical meanacing sound of canine authority.

"Is *that* supposed to be a growl?" purred the cat. "I've heard more threat in a sick mouse trying to clear his throat."

"You needn't be rude!" I snapped. For a moment I forgot my fear and was justifiably offended.

But with no trepidation at all (which was rather insulting) the cat padded up and sat beside me. "You *are* lost, aren't you?"

Before I could think to stop myself—I don't believe in confiding in strangers—I had blurted out "Yes!" And I went right on to pour out my whole embarrassing story: coming down to New York, a walk to explore the neighborhood, then losing my way—how my panic gagged me—just *everything!* The mere memory makes me cringe!

The cat switched her tail. "Well don't worry, honey. A lot of us animals who live in New York—and most of the human beings too—are lost all the time anyway. Besides, I know where Charles Street is. I'll take you home."

"Oh, would you?" Yours truly heaved a sigh. "I'd be most grateful! I mean, even though you are a—a—"

"Cat?" she purred. "Don't worry, sweetie. If you find that too embarrassing, you can walk ten paces in back of me."

"Oh, I'd never do that! It would be, well, downright hostile, I think, not to walk side by side, since you're helping me. It would be downright—" I searched, as very often I do, for exactly the right word.

"It would be downright, all right," said the cat. "Come on—let's travel. My name is Irma, by the way."

"I'm Jerry," I said. "Jerome, to be precise. But my owner—Professor Thompson, that is—and the missis, they call me Jerry. Jerome is on my pedigree. Sometimes I think it's a silly name, however—"

"Into this alley! Quick!" said Irma. "There's a cop car at the corner. The policemen in New York take a rather dim view of stray animals."

"Oh dear! Oh my! This is what I feared most!"

Irma nudged me into a dusky space. While we waited for the

cop car to go, I could feel her steady eyes on my face. Piercing they were—but beautiful too: sort of greenish with flecks of opal and gold. (I know about jewelry from the missis's secret drawer in the bureau.) But it was as if that cat could see through my brown and white fur right down to what I really was. And still am. And always will be, I guess.

"You're a nervous soul, aren't you, Jerry?"

"Oh, no!" I didn't quite know how to take that appraisal. "As a matter of fact, for a cocker spaniel, I'm quite courageous. Not foolhardy, you understand—"

"Oh, perish the thought!"

"—but I have sufficient stamina to meet most of life's demands. And crises."

"Oh boy—you kill me!" Irma switched her tail again, with a certain disbelief, it seemed—although I could see no reason at all for any incredulity.

"It's just that—" I spoke very softly, and Irma leaned close, right into my whisper. "It's that there's one thing I fear above all."

"What's that?" She mimicked my apprehension.

"The Dogcatcher! It's a primitive thing—"

Her sudden laughter was so out-loud, so reckless and free, that I thought it would call up not only the dogcatchers, but all the cop cars in New York as well.

"Shhh! Shhh!" I urgently tried to warn.

"You kill me, babe!" Irma shook her head, and her tail flickered off to someplace amusing, and her eyes sparkled on me delightfully. "As if one cat's laughter could even be heard in the uproar of all New York. Come on—the coast's clear."

We walked down blocks, across streets—with the light, I insisted—and past the old houses of Greenwich Village, which at that time still looked much the same to me. Being used to Connecticut—I mean, trees, flowers, and plants and things—I sort of missed the feeling of growth. But then I wondered if buildings could grow. Of course, not like trees. But they can age, I finally decided, and ripen, like fruit, and get more beautiful. The color of the bricks gets mellow, and little tilts appear, as if the houses, like sleeping people, were shifting position: all sorts of subtle changes appear. And although the houses seemed similar—as naturally they would, having been built at the same time, ages ago!—there were interesting little differences. The molding above the windows was like, but *not* like, the one next door. The bricks were set in a different pattern, like, but not *exactly* like, the house across the street.

It was during this first, nervous walk with Irma, who pointed out many interesting things, that I came to realize how fine and distinguished, despite its noise and rushingness, this city really is. The wonder of New York filled my head. And it has never left. Despite all the ghastly things that have happened since then!

Irma asked me about myself, and I gave her a brief biography. When—after describing my pedigree—I came to the part about the professor and how sometimes he would take me to class, to please the kids, and how I would listen to all of his lectures on different kinds of philosophy—well, at that point Irma shook her head and murmured, "Mmm. Then that explains it."

"Aren't you interested in philosophy?" I asked, realizing, of course, I was speaking to someone with little education, or none at all.

"'Philosophy . . .'" Irma purred on the word. "I don't even know what that *means!*"

"Well—well, it means thinking, basically." I tried to explain in simple terms. "And the thoughts that all the Great Thinkers have had."

"That seems like a rather large subject," said Irma.

"Oh, it is!" I assured her. "But Professor Thompson is highly intellectual."

"Personally, I prefer to feel. I get tinglings in my skin and fur."

"Oh, I get those too. All animals do. But I also like to *think.* You never can tell when it may come in handy."

"Do the Thompsons have any kids?" asked Irma.

"Why should they?" I inquired. "They have me."

"Boy, oh boy," murmured Irma Cat. I could see she was thinking—primitively—but I couldn't quite tell about what.

"I provide companionship," I continued. "I do tricks, sometimes. I bark, sit up, shake hands on demand—although, to be frank, the tricks rather bore me. They seem sort of infantile, but the missis enjoys—"

"Here's Charles Street!" said Irma. For some reason, she seemed relieved—although *I* was the one who was lost. "Can a brown and white, curly philosopher remember the number of the house he lives in?"

"It's number seventy-nine!" said I. "And I've never pretended to be anything but what I am! A pedigreed cocker span—"

"Come *on!*" urged Irma impatiently. She led me down a dark and dirty little flight of stairs—my coat of fur got a bit sooty there—which led to a narrow corridor between two houses. There were fences on both sides. "Can you jump?"

"Of course I can jump! When cocker spaniels first were bred—I know this from my pedigree—in the Middle Ages, we were bred to jump. For hunting in meadows, fields, and other—"

"So *jump!*" shouted Irma. (A cat's shout is like a frenzied meow!) And she herself jumped, very gracefully, right over the fence to our right.

I have to admit—it took me two jumps. The first time, I missed and fell back with a somewhat undignified grunt. Come to think of it—that's when my coat got really dirty!

"Been putting on a little weight?" inquired Irma when, finally, I alighted on the other side.

"Are you insinuating that I am fat?"

"No! Perish the thought! But you do have a nice plump suburban tummy. This city, among its other virtues, is a great slenderizer of animals. Unless they're pampered. But come along, Husky, and catch your breath. We have to go through five backyards yet, to get to number seventy-nine."

"Why couldn't we just go up to the front door? I'd bark, and—"

"I travel by backyards," said Irma Cat. "Besides, I want to

check out—I mean, I look forward with a great deal of pleasure to seeing with my own eyes this lovely duplex the professor and Mrs. Thompson have rented. And especially the cellar. So jump, Jerry baby—just jump."

Due to shortness of breath from that first faulty flop on my tummy—which *isn't* fat!—I would have liked to rest a minute. And also tell Irma that I preferred not to be called "Jerry baby!" But she had jumped—just as if she had wings—so I had to go too.

Six fences there were before we reached the Thompsons' backyard. And they weren't the nice low picket kind that you find in the country! However, some were easier than that first one, due to boxes and—nasty!—garbage cans that were piled along the way, permitting halfway jumps.

"Oh my word!" I panted when, at long last, we had landed beside that convenient little tree in my backyard. "Oh dear— oh my—"

"A little winded, sweetie?" purred Irma. "You didn't do much exercise, did you, up in the bosom of lazy New Haven?"

"It's easy for you to talk," I gasped. "There were trees along the way. You could climb them and leap right over."

"You stick with me, pup. I'll have you climbing trees like a polecat."

"You certainly will not!" I exclaimed in an indignant woof. "For a dog—an authentic, self-respecting dog—to climb a tree would be—"

"This is it, eh?" Irma glanced around. "Mmm—very nice! Very nice indeed. The Thompsons have the first two floors?"

"Yes. And I heard the professor say that in the basement, which all the tenants have access to, there's a clothes washer, a dryer, and several other appliances."

"A public space—*mmm!* And look at that—a broken window, leading straight into the basement and all those lovely appliances."

"I'm sure if I call attention to anything imperfect—as well I can, since I sometimes act as a guard dog too—but I'm certain the missis will fix that broken—"

"*Don't you dare*—my fat furry friend!"

"I am *not*—"

"I'm very partial to broken windows!"

"A little overweight, perhaps, but—"

"Come on, skinny. Let's see if we can fit through the window!"

As a matter of fact, I didn't fit. (I'd been eating nervously since I learned we were going to move to New York.) But Irma did. And once inside—she's *very* agile—with one long claw she pulled the bolt and the window swung inwards.

In a moment we two were sitting together, surveying the basement. And right here I may as well admit that I have a lovely basement. It's always very nice and clean—and one senses taste, very good taste indeed, in the way all the fine appliances have been placed. Our George, the janitor of the Thompsons' building and several others on Charles Street, is short and friendly and very efficient. He does a good job. But he doesn't come into our story at all. So thank you for everything, George—and goodbye!

"It's really an excellent cellar," I decided. "If I were grading this basement, as sometimes I have heard the prof giving grades to his students, I would give it an *A*."

Irma said not a word. But I saw from her eyes, how they glanced here and there, and studied and appraised, that she too thought it was a grade *A*. Finally, with one of those charming tail-switches of hers—of course cat's don't smile, but it was as if her tail did a little grin in the air—she said to me sweetly, "Let us sit down, my darling dog—"

"I *despise* false intimacy!"

"—and chat for a moment."

I did as requested. Sat down, that is. As it turned out, Irma Cat did most of the chatting.

"It just so happens I'm in need of a pad. And I don't mean these!" She held out a paw and wiggled some pads.

What she meant was, she needed a place to stay. Well, naturally, I had a fit. My word! I got nervous. It would all end in tears. Et cetera. The very idea!—a cat in my basement! What would the neighbors—and the papers—say? Apart from the propriety—a dog giving shelter to a cat I'd just met—why, what would the Thompsons say?

But Irma reminded me, with that explanatory tail of hers along with her words, that probably she had just saved my life. The dogcatcher. Et cetera. (I love that expression—*et cetera!* It both opens and closes so much.)

In the course of that long afternoon I learned Irma's whole story. It seems that she was lost herself, although she knew all the time where she was. She'd been living with a couple—a couple of human beings, that is—called the Nussters, on the Upper East Side of New York, where, in Irma's exact own words, a lot of the people are "rich and dreary."

"But you can also be poor and dreary," I sagely advised her. "Philosophy teaches us that."

"So does life, furry-face. I've known several deadbeats who were also dead broke."

She went on with her story, which I found increasingly fascinating. As a little kitten, she'd been given to Mrs. Nusster by one of the lady's canasta partners—"so Madame Nuss would have something to do with herself when she wasn't playing canasta or looking at television," said Irma. "Or eating tuna fish sandwiches. It was 'Here, kittykitty!' and 'Pretty kittykitty!' And I can tell you, Jerry, my friend, this is one kittykitty who got pretty sick of jumping up in Madame's lap to eat the ends of her tuna fish sandwiches."

"I thought that cats liked tuna fish."

"Well, most of us do." Her tail snapped rebelliously in the air. "But I'm here to tell you, you are *not* looking at your usual feline friend. Mrs. Nuss had a passion for tuna on rye—which I happen *not* to share! And also I don't do tricks on demand! She tried to teach me a couple of things—which I would have none of, naturally. We just were not a *family,* that's all."

Through eyes that were both nostalgic and sad, Irma stared into space: the Mysteries of Tuna Fish, and the Family, and Tricks, were solved out there, somehow.

She'd already decided to "split," she said, before events took a crucial turn. (To split means to leave. It was somewhere in here, on that long afternoon, that I first began to realize that

Irma was going to add lots of new words to my already large vocabulary. Slang words, to be sure; but then, one can't always live on a college campus.)

The crucial turn was, Mr. Nusster decided to sell his business, which was manufacturing underwear. He had picked up a "condo," cheap, in Miami. (A condo's a condominium: a kind of apartment that a human can own. Sometimes Irma gets impatient with me, but I always insist on being informed of exactly the proper meaning of words, be they slang or technical terms.)

"And in this building, which specialized in sunshine, canasta, and shuffleboard, there were no pets or children allowed," said Irma. "So for heart-wrenching months the Nussters worried about what to do with the kittykitty here. But finally I'd had it up to my whiskers, and in a spirit of feline generosity I decided I'd do them both a favor. One evening, while they were watching *Mork and Mindy*, I wished them a fond farewell, finished the last of those vile tuna fish sandwiches, and sneaked off into the New York night—my own cat at last!"

Her opal eyes brightened at the thought of her daring on that night of nights. Then they darkened somewhat and became the color of maple syrup, which may be the color of serious thought. "The trouble is, I really didn't know where I was going. This happened only last March. Since then I've been more or less camping out. Thank heaven that it's still September and the weather is warm enough for stray cats!"

"And you haven't found a new owner yet?"

"I don't *want* a new owner!" Irma snapped.

"Well, but Irma," I expostulated, "an animal has to have an owner. Or otherwise how can it be a pet?"

"Now listen, my cockeyed cocker friend—"

"That *isn't* necessary!"

"—I do *not* want to be a pet! I didn't give up on the Nussters in order to spend the rest of my life playing the equivalent of cat's canasta! With *any* new owner!" Her tail thrashed: an exclamation point.

"Then what *do* you want to do?" I asked, after a silence I let extend so that peace could be established again. "Or what do you want to be, if not a pet?"

"That's just it!" As well as a grin and an exclamation point, Irma's wonderful tail can suggest a question mark. "I haven't decided yet."

More quietness passed between us. But not the bad kind: we were just thinking—separately, but together too.

"Well," I offered, with hope in my voice, "you'll think of something."

"Darn tooting!" said Irma. She knows how to swear, but I find her euphemisms much more beguiling.

"In the meantime, however"—that tail again: it snapped in the basement air— "this highly ambitious kitty does need a place to lay down her bewhiskered head. So how's about it?"

"I really would like to, Irma, but . . ." I enumerated the difficulties, both moral and physical. Our sharing the cellar, her getting in and out: it simply would not do! I employed reason, intelligence, and even Philosophy; Irma Cat would have none of any of them.

"How would you like to be free in New York?" Her eyes challenged me. "I mean *really* free! You—your very own dog! You would wander around all over the city. At liberty! No fear of the cops, the dogcatcher. Your very own turf—like a huge broad lawn—New York would be. Would you like that, my cockeyed cocker friend? Mmm? Would you?" Her opal eyes, her mezzo voice, her multicolored fur: she was tempting me. And she *knew* it, too.

"Well, yes, but—" By now I was coming to realize that my friendship with Irma was going to include a lot of buts.

"Just yes or no. Do you want to be your *own* master? Do you want to even try?"

"Of course, but—"

"Then let me crash here—I mean, rest up a bit—whenever I need to." There are moments in life—in a dog's life too—when the whole future hangs on the thread of a question. "Well? Will you?"

"Oh—all right."

"Thatadog!"

Before I had time to ask how my freedom could possibly be secured in the perilous metropolis, Irma dove into the trash can placed in an alcove under the cellar stairs.

I heard her scrabbling and scrounging around. "Irma, what—"

"One minute. Ah! Just the thing!"

She jumped out. In her mouth was a simple little brown paper bag.

"In *that* paper bag is my freedom?" I asked.

"Don't say a word!" she admonished me brusquely, and dove back in.

A shower of small and peculiar dry rubbish began to fly over the rim of the trash can. And how fondly I now recall all those objects! There were a crushed pack of cigarettes, some aluminum foil, a broken chain, the foot of a chair, and a largeish nail: all seemingly unimportant things that would grow to mean so much to me.

"That ought to do it." And out flew Irma herself, at last.

"And this junk is supposed to—"

"Just watch." Irma sprang a claw and tapped me warningly on the nose. "I now place this junk, very neatly, in the paper bag." Which she did. "And I fold the opening of the bag"— which she did—"as if a tidy human being had placed something of very great value within. You will notice, I hope, that all this priceless trash is dry and clean and not liable to rot, so that even the most fastidious mutt can not object to any of it. You *do* have a license?" She examined my collar and found what, naturally, I would not be without. "I might have known: bronze! Oh boy—"

"I *still* fail to see—"

"Then listen! And you will know," said Irma. She held up the bag and let it dangle from the claw of one foot. "So here we have this paper bag. Very proper. For all New York and the world to observe. Now bite the rim and hold it in your mouth."

"I will *not!*"

"You want this claw on that stubby little tail of yours?"

I bit the bag.

"And there we have him!" With a flick of her tail, like the

hand of a master of ceremonies, Irma Cat presented—*me!*
"Your typical domestic dog, sent off on an errand. To the
delicatessen, perhaps, for a dozen tuna fish sandwiches the
missis has ordered."

"Ug—glh—mmp!"

"Don't you get it yet? You crazy cockeared cocker, you! You're
being of service! With that bag hanging out of your open
mouth, you obviously are doing your duty. You're fetching
something. Contributing to Society. You see, Jerry baby, the
thing is this: in this city of cities you can go anywhere—a dog
can too—as long as he looks as though he knows where he's
going. You don't have to know—hardly anyone does—but you
have to *look* as if you did. So welcome to freedom!"

All I could say was, *"Ug—glk—mmp!"*

And that was how, despite my most severe misgivings and
my fear that it all would end in tears, Ms. Irma Cat came to
live with me.

TWO

Our Life
in the Cellar—
with My Appliances

It has often been said—or at least it certainly should have been said!—that a dog who takes a cat into his life goes adventuring in the unknown. The completely unknown in the case of Irma, because the more I got to know her, the less I understood that cat. Now I'm forced to admit that up in Connecticut I'd known only a few of the feline species, and mostly males, at whom I'd barked, as a proper cocker should. But that Irma—my word!

And in addition to Irma—around her, above her, below her, everywhere—was all of New York, which was really *new* New York to me. A place of enchantment, made out of stone and hard concrete. I know it is strange—and Irma would say it's downright freaky—but sometimes this whole vast city, New York, seems like a dream that I have dreamed up while asleep, and if I changed my position—or blinked—it would all just vanish, or change into a forest. The huge, tall buildings would become big trees—and the people, insects . . . but we animals would remain the same. That's what we do the best, you know. We don't change, like the human beings or cities.

For, after a few days of consternation—how I worried and fretted, during those days, when Irma prowled and the Thompsons were forced to leave me alone in the cellar—I made one or two trial runs with my bag. I discovered that right across the yard from the house where I and the Thompsons lived, there was a sadly broken-down fence that led to the yard on Perry Street, which is the next street, going north. And by nice good luck—but not *too* good, good luck, because excessive good fortune is worrying: it makes me feel something bad's bound to happen—a passageway led from that Perry Street yard to the street. In other words, I could be free and at large without jumping over those clumsy fences. Which I did, and still do, very clumsily. Irma's right—I *must* reduce!

So out I ventured, with my neatly packed-up paper bag held tightly between my teeth. The first run was only around the block. And was I ever scared! Not only of the dogcatchers. The kids were much less well-behaved than the ones I had known in New Haven, and everybody seemed threatening. But I made it round the block that first day, and felt very proud of myself.

Irma laughed, and said, "Congratulations, you madcap spaniel!" when she got home that night.

I began to tell her about my walks. How I'd find a little hidden park, a green oasis, surrounded by steel. They're like intimate whispers in your ear, these little green parks. And oh, so private—so personal! Or a building I'd found, just covered with ivy. And I like ivy. For some reason I don't care whether I ever understand, ivy always make me feel at home. And it makes me feel safe. It means something has lasted long enough for the slow-growing ivy to grow round about it. Then there were the showers, the dusky rain clouds that thundered together suddenly. But it's funny: in this biggest of cities, a shower feels like a welcome bath given by a good master. The water splashes down so fast, and you know it's well meant—and then afterwards you're clean.

But the most dramatic walk of all was one I took towards

sunset time. Because all at once, down one of the city's straight streets, a burst of golden light appeared. The West was aflame. I stopped—stark still. And I felt like a dog who'd been cast in bronze.

Irma liked my story of that walk. She purred her most mysterious purr—but she didn't say a word.

Irma's own life during those first few weeks was, to me, absolutely incredible. (Not that it got more believable later on!) Now I'd be the first to admit—no, Irma would be the first, I'd be second—that up to my move to New York my standards were rather conventional. ("Connecticut standards," Irma purred. "You really kill me, furry-face!") However, even though I was raised in New Haven, in the suburbs thereof, I pride myself on being broad-minded. But Irma's life—my word! To describe it would take an imagination with no boundaries at all. Which I almost do have, but not quite. When I'd said that she could use my basement as temporary lodgings, I'd expected that she would rest, exercise, eat a bit from what I could snitch from Mrs. Thompson's kitchen. But not Irma. She was up at the first light of dawn, which came through a crack in the dirty window, and out to "find herself." Well, she looked in some very strange places, is all this cocker spaniel can say.

It wasn't so much that she wanted a job. Most animals don't have jobs. I mean, some horses do, maybe, and a cow should give milk—but as a rule, which I'd tried to explain to Irma, without notable success, cats and dogs are just pets. Of course there are seeing-eye dogs, a group that I happen to respect very much, and police dogs too, none of whom I would ever like to meet, but most of us just want to give our love and companionship to masters. And get a little back, if we can. Irma wanted no master. She wanted to be her own boss and "find herself"—an endeavor she also described as "realizing my potential." In my own opinion, a lot of humans, and animals, spend too much time in "finding themselves." They often don't like what they find.

In Irma's case, this quest she was on had something to do with being Irma Cat to the fullest, and also, as she explained one night, with making a contribution—to the world, society, something quite grand. Philosophically speaking, I found this need in her rather fascinating, but in practical fact it didn't work out. The first two places in which she tried to "find herself," make a contribution, et cetera, were a Chinese laundry and a Greek restaurant.

(Somewhere in those days there was also an Italian snackery. The professor was walking me one evening—an unfortunate coincidence—and Irma crept by, just covered—no, *overgrown*—with spaghetti. I pretended not to know the dear, which bothers my conscience now. The prof, with many disdainful noises, tugged me away from this walking, dripping Italian meal. It was their first encounter, and led to many complications. At any rate her employment at Manrico's Blue Grotto was short, and somewhat disgusting too.)

The trouble was, in all these three establishments—the Greek restaurant, the Chinese laundry, Manrico's Italian snackery—instead of realizing herself to the full, she was only supposed to demolish mice.

"A mouse's just not the person I want to be!" said Irma the night that she had been discharged, by having a skillet thrown at her, from the Greek restaurant. "I get fond of those little furry guys with their beady eyes."

I had come to enjoy these nightly chats, when Irma came home and the Thompsons were safely asleep upstairs. They took place way past my bedtime, but I was living in New York now, with my bag—my "traveling bag," we called it—and I'd started to feel sort of spunky. I don't really know what "spunky" is, but I'd started to feel it anyway. In fact, the basement had become my almost-favorite place in the house. As I had suspected she would, the missis had cleaned it up very nicely and put a chair or two around, and a mat for me, so yours truly and she could relax together while she was doing the laundry.

"There's a nasty virus going around the mouse community," said Irma.

"Like what Lo Wing had?"

"Exactly!"

Lo Wing Mouse had been one of Irma's favorite rodents over

at the Chinese laundry. He'd come down with this very nasty virus, and Irma, to keep him warm, had bundled him up in a freshly laundered face cloth. It was this simple act of tender generosity that had provoked the owner to dismiss my friend by throwing a hot flatiron at her.

"Mikos Mouse got the flu too," said Irma. "And Zorba, the proprietor of Zorba's Delphic Oracular Restaurant—"

"Is *that* the name of it!" I was very impressed. (The professor had done one semester of Greek philosophy.)

"No, it's not. But I knew it would flip you, you bewhiskered thinker!" She had to have her little joke. (And the trouble is, I don't *know* when she's joking!) "It's called Aristotle's Felafel Parlor."

"I *know* who Aristotle was!" I said. "A Greek philosopher!"

"But do you know what a felafel is?"

I had to admit it. "No."

"So stop boasting."

As I made it my business to find out later, a felafel is only some kind of Greek sandwich—and *much* less important than Aristotle!

"Anyway," said Irma, "big potbellied Delphic Zorba caught me slipping poor Mikos some grape leaves stuffed with rice and raisins."

"Then came the skillet?"

"Yes." Irma flicked her tail contemptuously. "It missed by a mile."

I shook my head. "You seem to have an affinity for hot flying objects."

She laughed. At first I couldn't see at what. But then I saw: it was *me!* (I.) "Irma, why do you think I am ridiculous?"

"I don't think you're ridiculous. But I think the prof has got to you—and got to you too much. You use too many words."

"There are always several ways of phrasing a statement, and I prefer—"

"There you are!" laughed Cat. "Using *words.* The Professor *has* really got to you. I think he's a creep! Just the way he looks—"

"But he can't help it if he has to wear glasses, and sometimes forgets to comb his hair, and wears different colored socks sometimes."

"He can't help it, eh?" said Irma. "Just forgetful, eh? Well I'm here to tell you that, glasses or not, he's going to get run down by a tricycle—or something even worse."

I felt dejected. "I suppose you don't like my missis either." My lovely missis! She's only five feet tall. With brown hair—the color of my brown patches exactly—which she keeps cut short. And a dancingness to her step that makes me want to jump when I see her!

"Oh, she's all right," Irma Cat allowed.

"And Professor T too." I meant to defend them both, I did! "He's very human! Why, just last night"—this was a deep secret—"I saw him eat his peanut butter!"

"You *what?*"

"He has this lust for peanut butter. And often, in the dead of night, I hear him creep down—"

"And make a peanut butter sandwich?"

"No. He's dieting. *Always* dieting! So he avoids bread. But late at night he slips downstairs and dips his finger—his little finger—into the peanut butter jar. And then licks it off."

Irma chuckled—a sort of a gurglepurr—and did so, I think, in spite of herself. "That's most endearing, I must admit."

"And he also has a sense of humor. Up in New Haven, one night I was snoozing in front of the fireplace—and I heard this growl! I jumped up, barking! But it was the professor's stomach growling, digesting his dinner. Imagine—a simple human, natural noise—and I had barked at it. But Professor T laughed—and long and loud—and then he called me into his lap and petted me. And we had this wonderful family feeling. Because the missis—she petted me too!"

I hadn't meant to reveal so much. Confessions are always embarrassing. And *me* they embarrass most especially. I cringe as quick as I sneeze, in fact. So perhaps Irma's right: *have* I learned to think too much, I wonder? Oh well, a dog can't change his spots. Not that I would want to ever change mine; I've had too many compliments on them.

She seemed to understand, however, and gurglepurred at the thought of the domestic scene—me barking at the professor's stomach. "Just don't let him make you a snob," she said, "with those twenty-one syllabusters you use."

"I won't, Irmy—honest!"

"And *never* call me *Irmy!*" Her glare would have turned a tiger to stone. "Even more than 'kittykitty,' I loathe that vile nickname! *Yecch!* It was that and the tuna fish sandwiches that finally broke my back at the Nussters."

"I'm sorry—*Irma.* Honestly. I will never call you that again. It's just that—oh—we don't know each other that well. *Yet,* I mean—"

"Okay! All right! So let it drop." She took a long and luxurious stretch. "Now—what has my favorite bow-wow been doing lately? Have you found any fascinating fireplugs?"

"Oh, Irma!" Now *that* is another example of how little we knew each other in the early days. I would have blushed, inside my fur, if I'd known how. "I don't go around in search of fireplugs!"

"Well how should I know? I'm not a dog."

"As a matter of fact, though"—as a matter of fact, I was really most eager to describe my latest accomplishment—"I walked over, almost, to Sixth Avenue."

"Good gracious! Next week it'll be the Bronx."

I thought about that. "No. Never the Bronx."

"Well, maybe Fourteenth Street. That's the northernmost boundary of Greenwich Village."

"In a month or two, perhaps." Ignoring the dig—it happens that Fourteenth Street is quite near, which I did not fail to recognize—I went on, "If it hadn't been for the sound of a fire engine—there's a firehouse on Tenth Street, you know—I would have made it all the way. But sirens unnerve me. And then too I wanted to get back home in time for the dryer."

She looked at me strangely. "The what?"

"The dryer. Mrs. T was doing the laundry today, and I've always enjoyed the clothes dryer."

"My word! Tell me more. Or as someone I know might say,

pray do go on. Elaborate. Expatiate! Let it all hang out, baby! *Why* do you like the clothes dryer? What fascination does it have for you?—you nut of a mutt!"

Must I admit it? (Yes, I must.) Her ridicule, which she always delivered with those wonderful high spirits of hers, had begun to delight me. I decided to share yet another confidence with her. "I love appliances, Irma!"

"You do?"

"If they behave. I mean—I love them selectively."

"Boy, oh boy!" said Irma Cat.

But it was too late to stop me now. "For instance, I *hate* the dishwasher—at least the one down here in New York—but I most enjoy the clothes washer and, especially, the dryer."

"Please explain to me the difference between these machines," purred Irma patiently. And her voice sounded, sort of, as if the very next thing she might do would be to call a veterinarian.

"It's how I feel—deeply!—about human appliances, Irma," I said. "Back up in New Haven I liked them all—the dishwasher, the clothes washer, and the dryer too. They were all so useful. And upstairs too. And beautiful too. They worked and worked —and they stayed in place. That's very important for an appliance, I think: to stay in its proper place."

"Oh boy—"

"But down here in New York the dishwasher in the kitchen upstairs has to be rolled to the sink and attached to the faucet, then the water turned on—and I keep on thinking, oh, it'll break! It'll break and the water will spill all over the missis's nice kitchen. I just do hate that rolling dishwasher! It makes me so nervous. But here, in the basement, the clothes washer is in its place—it never moves—and the dryer also stays where it should. I think I even like the dryer better than the one in Connecticut. Because it's white—and that one was green. And you see where my mat is?"

I padded over and showed her how I lay down. "There's a little leak in the dryer door, and the nicest, warmest breeze comes out. I think the missis must have guessed, because she put my mat right here. I just love to lie here and listen to the

laundry going round, and round, and round, and feel that little warm wind on my face."

"Oh wow!" said Irma. "*Bow-wow!* You really are something else again!" That look on her face had grown stranger and stranger. I thought, if she wasn't going to call the doctor, perhaps she had been deeply moved.

"You don't think it's unhealthy, Irma—do you?" I asked her very seriously. "If you think it's unhealthy, I will certainly—"

"Jerry—Jerome—I think it's terrific!" she yowled enthusiastically. "Imagine—grooving on a clothes dryer!"

"Oh, Irma—" That made me embarrassed. As usual. And as I've said, a dog can't blush, but sometimes we get the prickles. At least I do. "It isn't 'grooving.' I don't even know what 'grooving' means."

"It means tripping—"

"I don't know that either."

"Believe me, love—you were grooving, tripping—*enjoying* yourself—like on great music—on this miraculous clothes dryer! And that little warm wind. There is more behind that tear-stained face than I'd ever suspected."

"It isn't tear-stained," I explained. "Those marks beneath my eyes are really very natural. They have nothing to do with emotions at all. Indeed, as a breed we cocker spaniels—"

"All right! All right!" She snapped her tail. "Just stop with the dictionary definitions—you jerk!"

Something animal—and bad—had happened. We'd had a warm moment—almost as warm as the lovely zephyr that flowed from the dryer—but then Irma got angry.

I thought, right here, to smooth things over, I might propose an idea that I'd had. And it's strange, how often the good ideas of a person who thinks as much as I do turn out to be bad.

"Irma—if you like the cellar—"

"I do!"

"Well—I was thinking—a man has a dog, but the missis, she might have—"

"A kittycat?" Irma's tail lashed my face. "Named *Irmy*, perhaps? *His* and *hers?*"

"That hurt!"

"Forget it!"

She has a real temper, that cat of cats. Oh, does she ever! . . . I'm still not sure that I understand her. . . . I'm still not sure that I want to try.

THREE

Irma's Various Vocations— and a Bath

Well, as it always does, Time went on. In fact, that's all Time ever does—a point the professor made one day in his philosophy course at Yale. It gave me a queasy feeling to hear that. But Irma went on too—so did I—and I try not to think about Time too much. It's not good for a cocker spaniel's coat.

After her notable lack of success in the Chinese laundry, the Italian snackery, and the Greek restaurant, Ms. Cat decided to try something much more adventurous. In a way I was somewhat responsible. It was my own—altogether innocent— fault, my having made mention of the firehouse on Tenth Street. That very night, as we were chitchatting—I had even induced her to lie in the lovely little wind that blew from the clothes dryer—Irma suddenly burst out, "Say, that's an idea!"

Her whiskers crackled as she did a cat stalk all around the cellar. "Jerry baby, tomorrow I walk you all the way over to Sixth Avenue!"

"Why Irma, how nice!"

I was touched by her generosity. Until, next day, as she and my bag and I were strolling down Tenth Street, she stopped dead in front of the firehouse. "Will you look at that! It's just as I thought."

In front of the building, sunning themselves, were two old-timers. One was a dalmatian. He was all stretched out on the nice warm sidewalk, a delectable place for a dog to lie, and snoozing most contentedly. The other old-timer, also snoozing, was a fireman sitting in a chair tipped back against the front of the firehouse. They both seemed to be quite over-weight, and any passerby could tell, from the comfortable way they were sharing a nap, that they had been friends for many years.

"Take a look at that mutt," said Irma, with rather amused disdain. "I'd hate to have to depend on him if my litter box ever caught on fire. That is, if I had a litter box, or any such other domestic trap."

"Irma," I reprimanded her, "I may not be a dalmatian myself—and am not nearly as pudgy as that plump soul—but as a dog, it is very offensive for me to hear—"

"He needs to be retired!" declared our Cat definitively. "That's one firehouse that needs a new mascot."

"*You?*" I could hardly believe my ears. "Why—why—dalmatians are always the mascots—tradition, you know—"

"A ridiculous and outmoded custom!" announced my opinionated friend. "And also anticat. You run along home now. I'm going to go over and make myself irresistible."

"*Alone?*" For a moment panic raised my hackles. Anger usually raises dogs' hackles, but fear and terror—and lots of other things—can do it for me. "You walk me all the way over here, and then leave me alone?"

"Just hold that paper bag in place—and watch out for the dogcatcher."

"Don't joke like that, Irma!" I urgently pleaded. "I can't tell you how nervous it makes me feel."

"You're four blocks from home!" she meowed me loudly. "Now be a big bow-wow and go!"

"This will all end in tears!" I said, and meant. For a dog can cry, you know. At least this one can. I'm not so sure about cats, however.

But I went. (And made it safely home, I am happy to report!) And the last that I saw of my madcap cat, she was marching across Tenth Street, tail held high, about to become irresistible.

She was gone for three days, during which I pursued my excursions with bag.

Then, one morning—a Wednesday morning it was, I believe, and the missis had done the laundry early—after breakfasting in the kitchen upstairs with the missis and Professor T, on my way to the basement I thought I smelled smoke.

Now a dog has several kinds of barks. There's the welcome-back-master-have-you-had-a-nice-day bark. It's your friendly woof-woof. There's the please-may-I-have-some-more-supper bark, which is sort of a sly whine, and meant to be very ingratiating. On the more disagreeable side, there's the what's-that-I-think-I-*think*-I-hear-a-strange-footstep bark: the burglar alarm. It contains a throaty warning growl. However, the most distressing bark of all is the *fire-fire!* or *I-smell-smoke!*

As I made my way, with mounting fear, down the cellar stairs, I was prepared to give my all: just *howl* for the fire engines to come! But rounding the corner into the basement, expecting to be confronted with flames (at least with a smoldering rag or two), I saw come creeping out from behind the clothes washer my friend herself, Ms. Irma Cat. She was singed beyond recognition, almost. Her fine hair had gone crazy: it was tufted in clumps and was jumping off every which way. She was dreadfully dirty, all sooty and *yecch!* And the awfullest thing of all—most scary, I mean—she gave off this terrible smell of fur burning.

"Oh Irma!" I gasped. "How ghastly! What happened? My word! Were you caught in a fire?"

"No, sweetie," purred Irma, "I got this way just from sniffing catnip. *Of course I was caught in a fire!*"

Most colorfully, Irma described to me what had happened, while with my assistance she took a bath. (As a matter of fact, that was the second most wonderful bath in my life! The first occurred when Mrs. T was making pancakes and spilled the syrup all over me. Oh, maple syrup! The bath afterwards was delicious and divine! I still have sweet dreams about that bath.)

Next to the clothes washer there is also a sink—a deep sink, a kind of scrub-me sink—with a shelf beside it. I jumped to a chair, to the shelf, to the sink, and nosed the faucet until warm water—and Irma had to be satisfied: not too hot, too cold—was spurting out. Now I know most cats like to lick themselves clean. But the mess my friend had made of herself could only be cleaned by water and soap.

Quite a lot of soap too, because I spilled the Woolite. Her fur being so exquisitely soft, I had chosen Woolite over Tide or Oxydol. That spilling made her mad—at first. She began to laugh then—and then so did I! Then, to prove how mutual life can be, she whipped my forepaws out from under and I fell in the sink—and for quite a while we had a lot of sudsy fun.

That was the first time I took a bath with anyone. Apart from the missis—with the maple syrup. And you can't count that; we both tried to be reserved. But this time—my word!—it was a cat! And such a cat! The doglike splashing! Life really can be hilarious. And instructive too.

It seems that at the firehouse Irma did make herself irresistible. Even Jake, that potbellied dalmatian, was won over completely. He had given up riding the engines himself many years ago, but he said that if Irma was crazy enough to try it once—well, go ahead. So at the first clang of the fire alarm—a sound I myself find very disturbing—up Irma jumped, in the driver's seat. The firemen all thought that was cute. . . . Poor humans—little did they know!

"My first blaze I just watched," said Irma, rubbing detergent over her paws. "It was only some trash in a vacant lot. But last night we had a five alarmer."

"Oh dear—oh my!"

"Stop saying, 'Oh my!'" She splashed soap in my eyes. "It was a warehouse—empty—"

"Thank heaven!"

"—on the Lower East Side. But they wouldn't have *known* it was empty except for your very own kittycat here. Since I couldn't handle a hose—but I tried!—I decided to search for possible victims. Of course the place was locked, no lights, surrounded by parking lots—"

"So it *had* to be empty."

She dug her claws into my back, which she happened to be washing just then. "There could have been someone *trapped!* I leaped from the rear seat of the lead engine, raced into the flaming inferno—"

"And no one was there—"

"You wash your own fat suburban back!"

"Please go on. Irmy—*Irma*—please?" The truth is, I was enjoying her story. And also I found it most pleasurable to have a cat scrubbing my back.

She resumed the scrubbing—and the story too. "There was no one there. I made sure of that. Looked in every room. But just as I was coming out, the roof caved in!"

"Oh my! My word! Ouch! Irma—please—your nails. I know you're excited. A little to the left now. Oh—that's wonderful! That's heaven. Go on."

"I was trapped. Outside I could hear the big fire chief saying, 'Where's the cat?' They realized I was still inside." Irma stopped her massage, much to my annoyance. But I spoke not a word. She obviously was very moved by the firemen's loyalty. "And Jerry—you should have seen those guys! They tore down the door, where it had caved in, and came charging through the flames—just for me. I really wasn't in all that much danger—some soot and some sparks—"

"How frightful!"

"—but I'm sure I could have got out. But those guys, Jerry—gosh, I love firemen! They charged through the fire— they gathered me up—they lifted me to safety—"

"I thought you said you could save yourself—"

"Will you *listen*—please! They fondled and they comforted

me, all the way back to the firehouse." Her voice dropped off suddenly—*kerplunk!*—like someone who'd backed off the edge of a roof. "Then they put me in a cage."

"They did *what?*" My bath seemed of less importance now.

"Yeah. This Big Ed—this gorgeous guy of a fireman!—said, 'Dis cat is nuts! We gotta lock her up.'"

"Oh *no!*"

"Let's rinse," said Irma. "The first chance I got—they were feeding me milk—to help me over my fear, they thought—I split from the firehouse.

I nosed off the faucet.

"Too bad," she murmured. "I really got hung up on firemen."

I mumbled a few condolences. Although I was secretly glad that she had been separated from "Big Ed," to whom, it seemed to me, she'd been developing a somewhat unhealthy attraction. I suggested, to ease the pain of separation, that the nicest way to dry ourselves would be in my favorite breeze. Which we did. And that was the first time I ever allowed a cat on my mat. But there, in the delicious wind, we rested together comfortably.

For almost a week that captivating cat and I lived quietly in the Thompsons' basement. She wouldn't admit it, but I know that Irma felt rather embarrassed about the condition her scorched fur was in.

"I think I'll just lie low," she said. "For a little while."

Discretion demanded that although I knew the reason why, I maintained a tactful silence. She was a smelly mess! And I had to let the matter pass. You see, Irma Cat, for all her lust for adventuring, is really rather vain. And with very good cause, as I've pointed out. Her coat, which combines the very best features of several breeds, is absolutely spectacular—when unsullied by Italian cuisine and unsinged by burning warehouses.

For many days, despite her restless and roving nature, my friend seemed to be at peace. For one thing, the cellar was endlessly fascinating. Along with the major appliances there were several chairs, an ironing board, and a sofa in very sad shape. Its guts were hanging out, as Irma described it in her ruthlessly honest way. There were also two closets, containing old magazines, newspapers, a few children's toys, and some broken but mendable crockery, which previous tenants had left abandoned, alas. But there they lay, their separate pieces just waiting to be joined again. I find a sad poetry in such things, but Irma, after perhaps a twinge, calls on her sense of Reality and dismisses them as junk. We did some lovely browsing, however, in that one week—and walked out on occasion at night, with my bag.

Indeed, as I look back over it, after all the madness that followed after, that time seems like an interlude of sweet tranquility. But anyone who makes a friend of Irma Cat must be prepared to bid farewell to all tranquility and peace of mind.

The only unpleasant thing that occurred—and it really wasn't *that* bad, yet—was, we were discovered by the professor. And he and Irma, each probably recalling that first spaghetti encounter, confirmed their mutual hostility.

The prof tries to be a modern good husband and not leave all the household chores to the missis, so he came stomping down late one night to take out the clothes. I could tell that he had been studying, because his pipe was still clamped in his jaws. In New Haven I'd witnessed this scene very often: the missis would say, "Well, *are* you modern?" and the prof would mumble, "Oh, all right!"—and then he'd go off and do some chore, but preferably a little one. Tonight his chore was the clothes dryer. But there, on my mat in front of the dryer, he found yours truly and Irma, discussing some aspect of city life. As I remember, that night it was urban pollution. Irma said that sometimes her tongue got quite gray from just licking the soot off her! A dreadful commentary, I think, on our modern existence.

"Shoo! Shoo!" boomed the professor, who must have assumed I was keeping peculiar company. (It occurs to me now that he may not even have recognized this besinged creature as the same bespaghettied soul we had met on our walk. But she was a cat—and that was enough.) "Ah-*choo!* The [swearword] beast! Where did it come from?"

"He's allergic to your species, my dear," I hastily explained to Irma, and urgently signaled for her to depart.

She gave me a wink and flitted through the broken window. I wagged what little tail I have, barked most affectionately, and jumped up on the prof in a vain attempt to soothe his irritation away. He gathered the laundry, muttering unmentionables about all cats, and left.

And as soon as he was gone, my feline heroine returned. "The Great Brain and Peanut Butter Addict strikes again." She clawed up a sock, left on the floor, and held it out for my inspection. "Domestically he's not such a much."

"He was *thinking*, Irma! I just know he was thinking—about Aristotle, or Plato, or perhaps someone even more important. Although I don't see how *anyone* could be more important than Plato."

This was the first of several basement run-ins between the professor and Irma Cat. After each one he swore he was going to fix that dratted window. But of course he never did. As soon as he finished his little domestic chore—the laundry, whatever—he'd go back to his study, light up his pipe to help him think—as I lick my chops—and concentrate on philosophy.

As far as the missis goes, she saw Irma once or twice, at the start, but her own philosophy, which is less bookish than the professor's, just prompted her to leave well enough alone. If a cat or a dog—or a human being—doesn't irk the missis, she'd just as soon live and let live. Come to think of it, Irma's outlook and that of the missis are very much alike. They're both tolerant and easygoing—not sloppy, you understand, but lively, lovely creatures, that's all. (Must make a note: be more like that myself.) And also, not knowing Irma's concern for sick rodents, perhaps Mrs. T thought the kittykitty was keeping the cellar free of mice. Irma's tolerance does not extend as far as vermin—rats or roaches—however, and neither does mine!

At any rate, the broken dirty window never got fixed, and perhaps it was that—her way out into the world—that began to prey on Irma's mind. Her fur got rich and full again, her whiskers grew back, and I noticed the fidgets. For me, I was just content to be. And think. (In those days, *that* sufficed.) But

Irma began to stalk a lot, and prowl up and down. Not that I minded—with those long legs of hers. And how she stretched! —so yawningly and unfulfilled, with her forelegs extended in front of her. Nobody gets restless like a cat. And no cat gets restless like my Irmy.

"There's got to be something else!" she said.

"You want one of my Milk Bones?"

Whenever Irma talked like that, I felt like some dog who was little and insignificant, and living only inside myself. While Irma craved to live in the world.

Once, during those idyllic days, I told her how much I enjoyed just lolling with her in our comfortable cellar. She gave me one of her Irma smiles and said, "Sweetie, lolling is not an occupation." My littleness became even less. That's how I learned to keep quiet, with Irma.

Her walking, stalking, stretching, yawning—a human being would have been biting her nails—became almost unbearable. I felt as if I was coming down with ticks myself. I mean nervous twitches, not those nasty little insects dogs get.

"Please, Irma," I implored one day, "please just sit down. I simply can't endure—"

"The police!" she exclaimed. Inspiration—alas—had struck again. "Maybe they could use me!"

"Solve crimes?" I couldn't believe my ears.

"Be a help," said she. "The cops need comfort. It says so in the newspapers. Our idiotic, beloved mayor says that cops are abused. Make it up to them. They need someone—"

"Well, so do I. You comfort *me*, Irma—by, well, just by *being*."

"There's a station on Charles Street!" declared my comforter. "The biggest and best in the Village." She was loping, all purposefully, towards the window. "So long, furry-face—I'll be back! Perhaps."

A flash of eyes—a flash of tail—a shadow that flashed through the garden outside—and Irma was gone.

Yes, gone—for four dull, lonely days!

And if lolling wasn't an occupation, this moping certainly wasn't one either. I simply was desolate. I had grown so used to her purrs and meows, the grace with which she filled the basement, just slinking around the appliances. The broken sofa felt bereft. The chairs were a nuisance. The place wasn't mine anymore—which was strange. It was only a room full of useless junk. I was all alone, despite the professor and Mrs. T. I was lonely, at home.

But then, abruptly, Irma returned: not scorched, not covered with spaghetti or moussaka—but with a most woebegone face. In fact, she was very well fed, and thrillingly silky—but *what* a sad countenance!

"Oh Irma!" I said. "I almost would rather see you besmirched. What is it? Did they try to arrest you? In the Charles Street Police Station?"

She stared at me tragically. (And tragedy, I was soon to find out, is the saddest of all sad things.) "I just have broken a handsome—and an honest—policeman's heart."

It had been another one of Irma's mad dashes into life. The reckless soul! I lick my chops to admit it—but sometimes I really do envy her.

"His name is John," she began poetically. "*Big* John."

"Like 'Big Gorgeous Ed'?—the fireman?"

"This is New York, baby!" She snapped her tail. "And a lot of the guys here are big! Especially the ones attracted to me!" And then she resumed her reverie. "John Somethingorother. An unpronounceable Italian last name. He lived with his mother for years and years, and then—ungratefully—she died. Just last month. I could tell right away, as soon as I sauntered in, there was gloom all over the police station. Because all Big John's buddies were sad for him."

"But did the policemen accept you?" I asked.

She glared at me—at first with anger, and then with her very own Irma contempt. "Yes, sweetie," she purred. "They accepted me. As a matter of fact, I can safely state: no cat in New York has ever sat in as many blue laps as I have. Or been fondled, and petted, and called kittykitty—*yecch!* how I hate that name!—by New York's finest as I have. Anyway, the blueboys decided that I was exactly what Big John required. To distract him from his sadness."

"Very thoughtful," I murmured.

"Yes, thoughtful," mused Irma. Sweet sadness was flooding her. (I had almost had it up to my knees.) "And kind and humane. You know, there really should be a Humane Society for human beings too. But run by us animals. *We'd* be humane, you can bet! More than them." The melody of maple syrup returned to her voice. "So I cuddled up to Big John—as tender as a cat can be. And—" Here Irma's eyes grew large and sad. And a little peculiar, it seemed to me. "And then Big John fell in love with me."

"'Big' Ed—now 'Big' John?" I woofed somewhat sarcastically. And perhaps somewhat too persistently. "Do you always choose your human companions by their mere size, my dear? Or their weakness?"

"*Have you no heart?*" Irma fairly shrieked at me. "Here I am, telling you all about how this magnificent policeman's life had been darkened—his mother's death—he falls in love—and *you* just want to know, why 'Big' John? He happens to be at least six feet four! Which you're not!"

"That's pretty big," I had to admit.

"Yes! And with ravishing black Italian hair!" Irma growled. (I would have been proud of that growl myself.) "Going gray at the temples. And much more attractive than *some* hair I've seen!"

"Pray do go on," I requested—my aloof woof. "And let us both try to avoid petty digs. Although it's a known fact that scratching comes much more easily to some species than to others."

"Yes, let us both do that!" said Irma Cat. "And let us both also try very hard to avoid being pompous jackasses!"

"*Really!*"

"Anyway," the cat rumbled, "after falling in love, Big John wanted to take me home. In a cat carrier, if you please. He bought me my very own cat carrier. And in I jumped, to make him happy—and you know how I feel about being confined! Thence up to Twenty-third Street and Eighth Avenue, where Big John and Mama Unpronounceable had lived. A very nice apartment too, but one could see, half empty and sad. His

mama's old-fashioned things were there—like doilies and stuff—and then there was Big J's own equipment, like a roomful of enormous iron weights, which he lifts to give him strength."

And bulging muscles, I privately pouted. And a slender waist. Aloud, I merely commented, "How sad! The poor, huge soul."

Irma paused in her narrative—and not as if sadness had overcome her. More as if she was peeved, in fact.

"Well?" I prompted helpfully. And hopefully.

"He just wanted to look at television!" The Irma truth blurted out of her. "I mean—okay—I was sorry that he was sad—and one or two shows, well and good—but night after night—the *tube?* Just imagine: a beautiful guy like that, doing nothing but staring at television."

I had my rather spiteful relief and simply asked, "What happened?"

"I followed him back to the Charles Street Police Station. But no luck. When I'd jump in the squad car, ready for action— excitement!—the fight against crime!—they'd lock me up in Big John's Cat Carrier. Then, after the lovely lug got off duty, back to Twenty-third and Eighth, and more *Charlie's Angels.* And I'm telling you, Jerry, there's only so much *Charlie's Angels* an intelligent cat can take."

She came to the *really* sad part now: the heartbreak of humanity. It is called tragedy, as I found out later. See chapters eleven, twelve, and thirteen.

"We had to part," sighed Irma Cat. "As he slept one night— and boy, he is long: his feet hang right over the edge of the bed—I took one last look and meowed in his ear, very softly, of course, for him to remember—and I left."

"That *is* a sad story, Irma," I had to agree. "Almost as bad as getting singed."

She looked at me with her radiant, wise eyes. "There are things worse than hair to get scorched."

"How true," I nodded, since I knew she needed to hear me agree. (But personally, I think fur on fire is the absolute *worst!*)

Inside my heart, although I truly did pity Big John, I also was glad that they had had to break up. It meant that she had come back with me. For the next few days we chatted, had baths, and took walks together. The weather was lovely. It was autumn at its most glorious. (Did I tell you all it was early September—the sweet end of summer—when I and the Thompsons moved to New York? Well, it was.)

But now the world had rolled over into golden October. It wasn't the countryside, of course, but here in New York the few trees, in their lovely colors, seemed even more precious. Somehow the fall feels like the most robust season: we're bigger and stronger in the autumn air, with its husky, hearty, slap-on-the-back of a chill.

Irma walked me, with my bag, to Washington Square, and that was nice. All the students were scurrying off to their classes at the New School and NYU—just like back at Yale. I've always thought students are quite like dogs: they seem so busy, but carefree too—not all worn down, like a lot of adults. All in all, we had a few idyllic weeks. Yet during those days, so blessed by a strong sun above the vivid city, I could feel Irma's need to act—"to be part of the action," as she described it— grow stronger and stronger.

She did get her wish, of course—Irma always gets her wish— but in the most peculiar way. Along with becoming a part of the action, Ms. Cat became something of a star, indeed a celebrity, in the intellectual life—philosophers, students, teachers, dogs—that flourishes in Greenwich Village.

It was all so strange. . . . Sometimes I think that accidents, both good and bad, both planned and unplanned, happen more in New York than anywhere else.

FOUR

Irma and
Big Frieda

Frieda von Aknefrei just happens to be one of the foremost Egyptologists in the whole United States! But it took me a long time to convince Irma of that. However, I'm getting ahead of myself. I rather like to get ahead of myself. It's really much better than letting *others* get ahead of *you!*

What happened was, one evening my feline friend and I were deep in talk about that law that forces an owner to clean up after his dog in the streets. And personally, I think that it's a grand idea! All we dogs do. Anything to keep the human beings neat. Of course Irma had to point out that cats don't need such legislation, being so much more delicate. But that's neither here nor there.

Anyway, in the midst of this conversation, down came the professor and Mrs. T. And with them was Frieda von Aknefrei, to whom they were showing the house. I'd already been introduced to her—all the prof had said was, "This is my dog," but, well, it was a quick meeting—one day at the New School. Frieda is an archaeologist, whose specialty is ancient Egypt. She and the professor had grown to be quite close. He's interested in everything—archaeology too. And naturally, so am I.

I would describe archaeologist Frieda as something of a monument herself. "Big" Frieda, I choose to describe her. (If Irma can call her friends "big," why can't I?) She is tall—in fact taller than Professor T, but perhaps not as tall as Big John— and wide and meaty, and very impressive in every way, with her hair pulled back in a tightly rolled bun. I once heard the missis discussing her with the prof, and he said that in Egypt, when she and her crew were digging up things and they came to a rock that no one could budge, Ms. von Aknefrei could usually lift it all by herself. I stand in awe of her. And I also stand out of her way.

"Oh Lord!" said the prof, when he saw that Irma and I were chatting. "There's that alley cat again!"

Irma glowered at him and didn't move. She had long since ceased to be intimidated. "Who does he think he's callin' an alley cat?" she whispered to me.

It is interesting, by the bye, that animals—at least the most intelligent of us—can understand human beings quite well. But they, poor souls, can't fathom us. (Make a note: more research needs to be done on this subject.)

But Frieda stopped dead in her tracks—in those enormous shoes of hers that always seem to me as if they'd just come from an excavation. She gasped, "That cat is exquisite!"

And I have to admit—she was perfectly right. Irma was sitting on her hind legs, forepaws neatly placed in front, with her tail, in an elegant curl, like the ribbon on some wonderful package, wrapped beautifully around her. Her fur shone like amber—like maple syrup!—and her eyes, both brilliant and mysterious, glowed with the radiance of two opals. I saw Irma then through Frieda's eyes—through the fresh eyes of some- one else: she was new, she was strange—and Lord, I was thrilled!

"She's Bastet!" gulped Frieda von Aknefrei, and clasped a hand on the vast expanse of her chest.

"Who's *that*?" Irma asked me.

"An Egyptian goddess," I explained. "Who had a cat head.

The ancient Egyptians worshipped their animals as gods, sort of. I believe they especially worshipped cats."

" *That* seems reasonable!" Irma observed. "And how did they feel about cocker spaniels?"

"You needn't be mean." I glanced away. But I had to suppress my laughter. Irma Cat makes me laugh. I mean, laugh quite a lot. And most often she makes me laugh at me—a sensation I'm not quite used to, yet.

"And *I* look like Buby Bastet?"

"Apparently. To Frieda you do."

"I must have her," moaned Frieda. She attempted to make a ladylike gesture, a delicate gesture toward Irma of need and want, with her huge right hand—but accidentally she hit the professor and almost knocked him to the floor.

"She's yours," said he, as he stroked his chin where it hurt.

"My whiskers she is!" Irma readied herself for a jump out the window.

"I shall take her to my class!" pronounced Frieda. "So that all my disciples can finally see what Bastet really looked like."

"Like whiskers she will!"

"But Irma! You look like a goddess."

"I look like myself! And that's all I want."

"Please, Irma—wait!" I put my paw on her paw. (That caused a queer moment, as I remember, and I took it right off again.) "Why don't you try it? The New School! For Social *Research!* Just think! Education—and archaeology—and students too. Bless their innocent hearts! You say you want to do something—well, then, just think: you'll be helping all those students of Frieda understand the ancient Egyptian gods."

She debated inside herself. Those opal eyes blurred. "I'll bet the firehouse was more fun—"

But in that instant of doubt, Frieda swept down with those ham-hands of hers and scooped Irma up.

I heard my friend yowl, as America's foremost Egyptologist lumbered up the stairs, "This is all your fault, you mutt! And it will all end in tears—as a pessimist I know always proclaims."

They were gone. *She* was gone. . . . To what future? I wondered, as I sat by my dryer. Enjoying the warmth.

* * *

For the next few days my hair was absolutely electric with curiosity. And that is far more nerve-wracking for a dog or a cat than for even the shaggiest human being. Where *was* Irma now? And what was she doing? Did Irma like school? That last question made the heart fairly cease to beat! My Irma was now attending a university—somewhat unwillingly, to be sure— but my word!

It was on a Tuesday I had my answers. I know it was Tuesday, because, preoccupied as I was, I still did my household chores. On Tuesday the missis waters the plants. And sometimes she spills and doesn't notice. I bark—but only politely, of course.

When the last philodendron had had its drink, I went down to the cellar. And there was Irma, stalking like a wildcat! I could tell right away, from her tense parade, that something was very wrong. Since knowing Irma, I've become something of a connoisseur of cats' positions. My favorite one is when Irma lies with front paws crossed, or tucked under. Then she's happy and relaxed. She was neither relaxed nor happy that Tuesday.

"Irma!" I burst out. "I've been so anxious!"

"Thieves and liars! Cheats and phonies!" Her pace grew even more furious. "That's all those boring collegiate types really are. You can give me a good-hearted cop, or a fireman who dropped out of school—" Her fuming took her breath away.

"What *happened?*" I asked.

"I have tried the Life of the Mind," Irma Cat stated flatly, "and I'm here to tell you, puppy dog, it's not all that it's cracked up to be. And the teachers are the worst!"

"What happened?" Naturally I felt called upon to defend an honorable and ancient profession, but I knew I had better let Irma explode before I defended anything.

"Big Frieda is a crook!"

My legs positively collapsed beneath me. At least my hind ones did. I knew that Frieda von Aknefrei had a string of the most important degrees in back of her name, and I simply couldn't believe my ears.

"Believe me," said Irma, "more goes into that monstrous pocketbook of hers than lipstick and nail polish!"

"Begin when you left here."

"When we left here—right! Before we reached Frieda's so-called home—a slovenly mess on Hudson Street, with a few very beautiful things—but more of that later—before we reached Big Frieda's hole, I knew the kind of a dame she was. She tried to pass me off as a fur piece! Oh, whiskers—" Her anger disintegrated. "I shouldn't be so mean!" And she laughed. "As a matter of fact, I thought it was very flattering to be hung around that trunklike neck and paraded as some kind of very peculiar mink. She is lonely, Jerry. She's a lonely phoney."

"The foremost Egyptologist?"

"Yes, sweetie. The foremost Egyptologist between here and Fourteenth Street is a lonely, middle-aged, old soul—yes!"

"Professors aren't *like* that!" I tried to protest.

"They aren't, eh?" sniffed Irma. "Well listen, my friend—here is one kittykitty who's learned a lot more about life behind the library doors than you will ever know! Despite all those lectures in pure philosophy that your boss drags you off to."

"And a *thief* too?"

"A thief." Irma's tail more or less retracted itself. "Or let's say—a very high-class borrower. You get into bad habits when you live all alone."

"Imagine!" I couldn't get over it. "And she's written six books on the ancient Egyptians."

"She should spend some more time on modern New Yorkers. Herself included!"

The story, as I could put it together from Irma's jerky narrative, interrupted by frequent comments and observations, philosophical and otherwise, was as follows.

At first, despite my friend's misgivings at having to live with a lady professor, they had gotten on famously together. Even Irma had to admit that Frieda's apartment—hole though it was—was endlessly fascinating. It was full of Egyptian artifacts—like statuettes and pieces of pottery and some chips of stone with old Egyptian writing on them called hieroglyphics. And then there was modern stuff too. Like Barbie dolls. And a hula hoop!

Irma mused a moment over the hula hoop. Big Frieda felt a strange tenderness for it, and touched it often. And looked at her Barbie dolls. "Toys," Irma sighed. "The poor oversized dear. She misses her childhood."

But I was far more interested in all the Egyptian artifacts. "Have you learned to read hieroglyphics yet? Those pictures on the stones?"

"No," said Irma. "And I'm not going to try. Besides, there wasn't time. I was too busy eating."

"Eating?"

"Sure. That's all Big Frieda does. Just study and eat. Lots of lonely people eat too much."

"Not tuna fish sandwiches," I hoped.

"No, sir! What grub! The first night she went out and bought all the best cat food in New York. A veritable feast—if you're into pet food, I mean. But by the third or fourth day she'd decided that I was really human—or at least an Egyptian cat goddess—anyway, that I understood her, which I do, and that I'd enjoy some human food, which I would. So we ate together —sumptuously! Frieda talked all the time, and I meowed— between mouthfuls."

This idyllic life—Frieda von Aknefrei and Irma Cat, two roommates on Hudson Street—went on for a week. Irma wouldn't admit it, but I even believe that she secretly enjoyed the classes in Egyptology. Because Frieda took her every day to the New School. At first it was only "to model Bastet. The darling!" said Irma. But then, I guess, for company. And the students all loved her. Just as *my* professor's students—if I may state this with all due modesty—have *their* own favorite pet. A cocker spaniel.

"That's how I learned she's a thief," said Irma, almost sadly now. "You know, there's a little museum at the New School."

"The professor has been there often," I said—and had to admit the bitter fact: "but they don't allow animals."

"They allowed *this* animal!" said Irma. "The guards thought I was some ratty fur piece Big F had picked up on Second Avenue. And it was there, in after hours, when she and I were all alone—just us and the wreckage of history—that I found out she was pilfering. She would slip a little statuette—zip!—right into her handbag—then out the door, with a nod to the guard and a cheery smile—as honest as ice cream! Then back to the apartment—and out the statuette would come, to be added to the most interesting collection of Barbie dolls and Egyptian artifacts on all of Hudson Street."

"And she *keeps* them?" Horror, deep horror, was all I could feel at the thought of an archaeologist who was stealing such treasures.

"Well no, not exactly." Irma's tail curled doubtfully. "That is—she keeps them for several days, and talks to them, along with her Barbie dolls—and then takes them back."

I didn't know which to be more aghast at: the fact that Big F—I mean, Professor von Aknefrei—talked to her statuettes, or that she talked to her Barbie dolls, or that she stole Egyptian artifacts and then gave them back. In the wonderment of it all, something totally unexpected burst out of me.

"Oh, I love New York!" I shouted and barked. "Everything is just so—*unlikely* here!"

Irma gave me the kind of grin and/or smile that only the slyest of cats can flash. "It's gettin' to you, furry-face—the city is—isn't it?"

"Yes!"

We shared a silent shout of just pure joy and excitement and—well, a swelling of the heart they don't feel too often back in New Haven. You can't talk about things like that out loud, though. It cuts the experience off like a flower.

Irma started to stalk once more. She sauntered all around the cellar. I could tell she was feeling repentant even before she gave herself a lash with her tail. "I shouldn't be angry. The poor old bag! No one to talk to but students and statuettes. And her clothes—oh, Jerry!" A laugh changed her mood. "I have been in some of the rattiest shops on the Lower East Side, and I

never—no, *never*—have seen such rags! And her perfume—
oy vey! You know what even happened once?"

"What?"

"She was wearing me, as her fur piece, to class—to try to
impress the kids, I guess—and I think she was so obsessed
with Egyptology, she forgot that I was alive. You know how
professors get with their subject. Well, in a fit of describing the
Eighteenth Dynasty she yanked me off and tossed me on the
desk—as if I *was* just a stole!"

"Oh no—" I was starting to laugh.

"That isn't the worst, though. There I lay, and I didn't
budge—not wanting to cause embarrassment to Madame
Professor. But the reek of her terrible perfume—which smells
like a combination of vanilla extract and the Hudson River
—began to overcome this cat. I held my breath, tried to
concentrate—just think of anything else—but I sneezed!"

"Oh Irma!" I laughed so hard my whiskers got wet.

"So that was how the kids found out that Madame's fur
piece was really *real!* But she passed it off—she's not stu-
pid, you know—by laughing herself and telling them all
that she'd brought me in to show them what Buby Bastet
looked like. So I preened and did my Egyptian act, and the two
of us brought it off together."

For a moment Irma simply mused, meditating on the
strangeness of the ancient Egyptians and Frieda von Aknefrei,
and how it felt to be hung around a human being's neck.
Her eyes, in their thinking, seemed distant. "I don't think I'd
even resent too much being used as a stole, if it weren't for
that perfume. Or if it had been Big John the cop who was
wearing—"

She paused.

"Irma? What?"

"Just a minute. Wait!" Her stalking grew purposeful.

I couldn't see what needed waiting for. "Is that all of the
story?" I licked my chops expectantly, since I hoped there was
more.

"Just *hush!*" She was deep in thought. *"Mmm!"* came the
purr of her cat's brain, working. I didn't know what she was

thinking, but it sounded exactly like the hum of a fine-tuned computer or perfect electric clock.

"Irma? IRMA!"

"Big John and Big Frieda!" Her idea exploded. "It's a natural combination! If she'll change her perfume!"

"Oh, Irma—" I tried to be gentle but firm.

"Well, why not?"

"—I've heard about cats like you—"

"She's lonely—he's lonely—"

"—and I don't like everything I have heard."

"—they are both—not young. Their hair is getting gray. His mustache is beautiful, but it *is* getting gray. I'm sure they're both forty."

I had to admit, "That *is* somewhat past the age of consent." (Apologies here to those who—well—)

"Listen, sweetie—with us—us animals, I mean—it may be six or seven or eight. But after forty the human beings are all the same. I acquired this wisdom from Mrs. Nusster, when she took me to the beauty parlor. Big John spent the very best years of his youth taking care of his agéd mother. And Frieda spent hers studying—and then stealing and talking to statuettes. It's time someone brought them both to life. While there still is time!"

"Oh, but Irma," I expostulated, "to meddle like this—one incurs a responsibility."

"I've incurred worse than that. But you're too young to know."

The best—and only—thing I could do was to gather my hind legs under me and sit. And then wait. And lick my chops a little—to think. "I *must* advise you," I said at last, "I have the most severe misgivings—"

"Well honey, you take your severe misgivings and tuck them behind your long left ear! I have an *idea!*"

"As I feared," sighed yours truly.

"Did you ever play catch?"

"You mean, throw and catch? Like a ball or a branch? I *did* play that, Irma, when I was a pup. But I've more or less outgrown—"

"You are going to play it again!" said *The Cat.* "Only guess what it is you'll be catching this time."

"I shudder to think!"

"An antique—Egyptian—statuette! Quite priceless too. Just borrowed from the New School!"

"Oh my word!"

FIVE

Archaeology—
and Crime!

Hudson Street is a dingy kind of nondescript thoroughfare in Greenwich Village that doesn't seem to amount to much, but then at last it has good luck: it turns into an avenue. Eighth Avenue, to be sure, which isn't exactly one of the best—not Fifth, not even Madison—but at least it's not a dreary street. It was on Hudson Street, just as it lurched to the right, to become Eighth Avenue, that Frieda von Aknefrei had her apartment.

I never did get inside that apartment—"the hole," as Irma called it. (But it sounded to me like a hole full of treasures.) And often—how often!—I wished that I had. To hear Her Cattiness describe it, the rooms were bulging; and not only with borrowed artifacts. Big F had photographs of her friends, all covered with the dirt and dust of important excavations; a few lousy carpets she'd picked up cheap; an antique clock that worked whenever it wanted to; varieties of exotic perfumes, *all* of which smelled as if they too had come from strange excavations; the Barbie dolls; the hula hoop—well, I can't go on. It sounded to me like the fascinating repository of a frustrated but brilliant life. . . . Perhaps in the future—and all the philosophers say there is one—I can get inside that apartment. I would *love* to!

My job, however, was not to be in Big Frieda's apartment. I was supposed to stand outside, beneath the fire escape in the garden, and catch an invaluable wooden statuette of the Great Goddess Bastet in my mouth! (Just the thought of it, even now, makes my fur curl! It really does.) This statuette was even more utterly irreplaceable than anything else that can't be replaced because it was wood. Wood doesn't last as long as stone or bronze or anything else that someone could make a statue out of. If it's kept dry.

Irma's scheme was this. (And *when* will Irma ever cease to scheme? I hope never, in fact—after all, so far I've survived.) She was going to drop this little statuette off the fire escape of the building—there were *two* stories down too!—and I was going to nip it right out of the air with my jaws. And especially carefully too. Because if it had been made of marble, it would have knocked my front teeth out. Then Irma, by making a fuss near where the statue should have been, was to call the attention of Ms. von Aknefrei to the fact that it wasn't there. The cops—in whom Irma, because of Big John, had great reliance—were going to be called. Big John himself, in his beautiful blue uniform, would arrive—to the sound of trumpets, I've no doubt! They would find the statue in the backyard, where I'd carefully placed it. (Oh, it all seems so ludicrous now! Almost human.)

And Big J and Big F would become best friends just because of this idiotic prank. She'd say, "Oh, officer—you saved my statue!" And *he'd* say, "So you got statues, eh?" (Really!) "I sure would like to see more of 'em—*yuk!*" (Or some other kind of intimate chuckle.)

In all honesty, I must now most truthfully state that after I'd heard these plans of hers—my doubts, my fears—well, these really *were* the most severe misgivings I'd had about Irma. Until later on. Bless her heart!—there's always something more rambunctious to come.

The "caper," as she called it, was planned for the first Thursday after my friend had come down with her plot. In her days at the police station, comforting Big John, she had learned what his hours were. And also she'd left the Nussters on a Thursday—good luck—and I can't remember what other reasons there were for a Thursday. Oh yes—I remember another one! Irma has a good friend, a hamster, who's the pet of a fortune-teller on Bleecker Street, which is right next to Hudson. And Zilaka, the fortune-teller, has always said that on Thursdays either the best or the worst takes place. And Irma—strange creature—could never bring herself to believe that the worst is possible. But I *know!*

So on Thursday, way past my bedtime, when the Thompsons and all the other good folk in Greenwich Village, of which there are a few, were asleep, Irma tapped with her claw on the broken basement window. I had slimmed down somewhat, but I still couldn't fit through the hole. However, with my front teeth—and there's no improving on *them*, let me tell you!—I was able to draw the bolt and nose the window open.

"The coast is clear!" Ms. Feline said, with spylike glee. She had been out scouting. "You ready for some excitement?"

"No! This will all end in tears—I know it in my bones."

"Just get your bones out of the cellar, you woolly little werewolf, you! And I told you before—your face looks tear-stained anyway."

Big Frieda's apartment was on the third floor, overlooking the garden, of a rather unimpressive building—not nearly as nice as the Thompsons'—near the corner of Hudson and Jane. I had no time to make any observations, however, because Irma by now was completely caught up in the foolhardy escapade. She flickered and flitted along through the shadows like the master schemer she wanted to be. Myself, I just padded quietly and wished, for that night, I was back in New Haven. A passageway led to the rear of the building, and there rose the fire escape, like a steel skeleton lifting up in the night. I didn't like the look of it, but then, I didn't much like the look of anything that memorable Thursday night.

"Just stay here now!" whispered Irma.

"I'm very edgy, Irma. I wish—"

"I wish you could just fold your paws on top of your head

and keep quiet! That's Frieda's bedroom window up there—
the one with the pink light."

Before I could ask—why pink?—she had skittered up the
metal ladder that hung from the fire escape. Then up to the
second floor . . . the third . . . she was at the pink window. It
was open a crack.

And suddenly I remembered something. "Irma!" I called. "I
forgot my bag!"

She whispered down—rather loudly for an about-to-be-
thief: "Well forget about it. It's too late now."

"But my *bag*, Irma! It's my paper bag! What keeps me from
being suspected—arrested—"

"*Will* you shut up?" Irma hissed. "You sould like a hysterical shopping-bag lady!"

That was a new phrase. And even in the most trying
conditions I always add to my education. "What's a shopping-
bag lady?"

"I'll explain it later! For whiskers' sake—just *sit* there! Think
philosophical thoughts. And *please*—be quiet!" Like a snake,
she slithered back over Big Frieda's windowsill and vanished
into the spooky pink.

So I sat. And did *not* think philosophical thoughts! I thought
about the Dogcatcher.

It's been a long time since I've whimpered—except maybe
now and then, to get some attention when all-out barking
might be rude or otherwise inappropriate. I'd whimpered at
the vet's last March, when I was about to get my shots, but that
was the last time. But down in the dark, all by myself, in that
cramped passageway—with *garbage* cans on both sides and
the ugly fire escape looming above me—I felt a whimper
coming on. But I stifled it with canine courage, for two reasons.
First, it might have attracted you-know-who. They're everywhere, with their trucks and nets! And second—most impor-
tantly—I didn't want Irma to know how scared I was.

Suddenly, from my spot amid the shadows, I saw Irma's
pink-silhouetted outline appear at the window. She put
something down, and then pushed and strained with her back
to raise the window a little bit more. Very gently she picked the

something up again and maneuvered it through the opening.

"You there?" she called.

"Where *would* I be?"

"Oh, I don't know. The dog pound—"

"*Irma!* Stop that, please! This is no time for jokes!"

"Here she comes!" said the cat.

"Wait! Wait!"

Until that very moment I had not understood the risks involved. But there above, on the very edge of the fire escape, sat Irma Cat and, in her paws, an exquisite little statuette of Bastet Herself, Cat Goddess of Egypt, the Cat of Cats! Which *I* was supposed to catch in my mouth! It is one thing to know what a plan may be—I mean, have it all neatly wrapped up in your head—and quite another to see it above you, hanging between Irma's two front paws.

"All ready?" she called down cheerily. "Here she comes!"

"Oooooooo!"

The howl came not from physical fear, I assure you. The worst I had to expect—and would probably get—was a knock on the head. It was just for the madness of everything—for Irma, for me, for the craziness we were perpetrating, there in an alley off Hudson Street.

I bounced here—I bounced there—to position myself. I gauged the speed of the Goddess who dropped from the fire escape. I opened my jaws—closed my eyes at the last moment—and *kerplunk!*—I caught her without so much as knocking a splinter off!

It was truly the most remarkable moment in *this* cocker spaniel's life! The ancient, elegant statuette was balanced lightly between my teeth. I felt as if I were holding History—*all* of History—within my mouth: a unique sensation, if ever there was one.

"Ya got 'er?" called Irma.

"I got 'er!" blurted yours truly, but still not daring to unclutch my jaws. Very carefully I twisted my head and set Bastet down, right side up, so she rested on her wooden throne—which was part of the statue—paws placed on her knees, and the halo of godhead around her cat's head. "Oh, I

got 'er, Irma! I really caught her. What a catch! Not a dent—
not a scratch!"

"For whiskers' sake," my dear friend hissed, "you sound like
some guy out in left field who just caught the fly that won the
World Series."

"No ball player *ever* made a catch like that!" I justifiably
declared.

"Just sit tight now," purred Irma. "I'm going to have a
controlled conniption and let the Big F know that her precious
Basty baby has disappeared."

While Irma concocted her fit upstairs, I took the time to
examine the statuette. It was even more beautiful than I had
imagined. The eyes were wide and staring, and made of some
gems that never would perish or decay. Oh, surely they were
the eyes of a goddess, and could see much more than the eyes
of mere man or cocker spaniel! In fact, they were sort of like
Irma's eyes—except hers were alive, and along with what an
Egyptian goddess's eyes see, Irma's also saw New York.

I was so intent on examining Bastet that only with my left
ear, so to speak, did I hear the commotion going on in Frieda's
apartment. There first had been a certain amount of extrava-
gant yowling, as Irma pretended to discover the loss—then
some very real and panicky yowling, of the female human
variety, as Big Frieda discovered it too. Then they yowled
together—Frieda's voice was much deeper than Irma's—
consoling one another, I guess. Then there was a spell of
almost-silence, while Frieda went into her other room and
notified the authorities.

I enjoyed this interlude especially. The light in the little alley
was bad, so I carried the charming and awesome statuette out
almost onto the sidewalk, but of course not where it could be
endangered. A slice of streetlight fell across it, and I had my
rapturous fill of looking, touching, loving.

I had just moved it back to the safety of darkness when the
squad car arrived.

Then I did begin to listen in earnest. And what I heard was
not reassuring. Frieda sounded all right—that is, she sounded

like your usual hysterical famous archaeologist who's just lost a goddess—but Irma sounded queer. Her meows were genuinely alarmed and alarming.

I sat there in my perplexity, and suddenly Irma appeared above me. She leaned way over the fire escape and didn't whisper—she fairly screamed: *"Get out of here!"*

"What?"

"Run! *Run!* It isn't Big John. They must have changed the schedule."

"My word!"

"Just *go!* This guy's a fat thug who's going to make trouble. I know him from the station house. A dumb klutz!"

"A police officer? And fat? And—"

"Jerry—run!"

"But Irma," I called up, "you never did tell me: even if it had been Big John, what was supposed to happen now?"

"I was going to come out here, meow, and point down there with a delicate claw, and suggest the [swearword] thing just fell out the window."

"Why won't that work now?"

"*This* bum wants to arrest someone! He's grilling Frieda right now." Irma's voice became pleading—a tone I had never heard before. "Jerry—*go!* Go now! Go fast. Go home! I don't want to get you in any trouble."

"I will *not* abandon this priceless artifact!"

"Oh my word!" said Irma. With genuine concern, I thought.

"Why—why—anybody could pick it up! I don't want to seem condescending, Irma, but I know a bit more about Egyptology—" A low moan came from her. "Well, to make matters short, I shall stand by this statuette until—"

I hadn't decided until what. Nor did I have time to decide. For during my declaration of loyalty to the arts and archaeology, that fat thug in the blue uniform—and Irma's description was perfectly apt—had come racing down the apartment house stairs.

A flashlight flickered—it pierced into the alley—it fell upon me as I sat beside the statuette, determined to guard it.

And I heard a hoarse voice say, "Dat's him. I've hoid about

mutts like dat. Dey are criminal dogs. Crooks train 'em to steal. Nab dat dog!"

Before I could so much as whimper, bark, howl about my innocence, two rough and uncouth hands had seized me. They yanked my collar too! And I was dragged off to a terrible place.

SIX

A Terrible and Modern Place

The Charles Street Police Station is truly and most emphatically a terrible and modern place! The *old* police station, also on Charles Street, which I had seen several times on my bag walks through Greenwich Village, had a genuine old-fashioned charm—big windows, portals, stairs leading up. It had now been turned into co-ops, or condos, or some other kind of modern apartments.

But the new one—my *word!* It is squat, flat, ugly, and altogether undistinguished, made of soulless concrete. And it looks like a jail. Which of course it is—but in my opinion such things are best disguised. I simply could not make myself believe that on such a nice street—so many fine and venerable old houses—there ever could be a place like that. However, being dragged, one isn't objective or in the mood to evaluate New York architecture. And that dreadful cop did actually drag yours truly all the way to the Charles Street Police Station.

The big lug's name was "Hooch." At least that was the nickname by which he was known to his fellow officers. And I suppose he has loved ones too—the loved ones of "Hooch"—somewhere, somehow, somewhy. But why did he have to drag me along, in front of the world, like that? Oh well, I guess the other officer had to stay in the squad car, to search for other criminals. "Other" meaning besides *me!* The shame of it!

If I'd had the chance, I'd have choked or gagged—at least I'd have coughed pathetically—but there was nothing I could do, not even breathe asthmatically, to attract the attention of passersby. If I'd known what lay ahead of me, I'd have *died!* But one can't have everything.

So on to that terrible, modern edifice: the Charles Street Police Station.

"Dis mutt stole a statue," said Hooch to the sergeant behind the desk.

"Uh-huh," the sergeant said, and then looked up from his work to study me a moment. "Lock 'im up!"

And yet the sergeant—Sergeant Mike Reilly—seemed rather a decent man. He had an impassive, guarded face—once handsome, perhaps—that had been made sad by seeing much too much sadness. In fact I've noticed that most policemen (Hooch very much aside) seem sadly resigned to see a tear-stained face. And my own was really tear-stained now.

They didn't lock me up, as it happened: too small to merit my very own cell. Instead they just tied me to the sergeant's desk; ignominious, but more comfortable. I walked my hind legs underneath and tried to appear invisible. It didn't work.

And so began my first—I hope my last—and so far my only—night in jail. I may say, it was one of my less welcome experiences since coming to New York. Indeed, it was the worst. It was awful! *Unimaginable!* I could feel pure panic, which is one of my more familiar sensations anyway, beginning to rise in my throat. It occurred to me—vain hope!—that if I howled loud enough I might waken the missis and the professor, although they were both of them sound asleep, and two blocks away at that! What madness there is in despairing dogs!

Foolhardy or not, the question—to howl or not to howl—had been decided affirmatively—yes!—my head was thrown back —when there in the Charles Street Police Station hope suddenly appeared. Irma and Frieda came galumpfing through the door. Or rather, Big Frieda galumpfed, with Irma tucked under her arm.

"Thank heaven! There it is!" Frieda charged towards the sergeant's desk, where Bastet was sitting quietly, surveying with great disdain the Charles Street Police Station. (The gods have all seen a lot.) My least favorite policeman—the one who had dragged me—had grabbed the statuette too and turned it over as stolen goods. . . . There she sat, as stolen goods and the Wisdom of the Ages too, on the desk of Sergeant Mike Reilly.

"Dat yours?" said Hooch, and gestured with his thumb towards the goddess.

Frieda dropped my co-conspirator, who fell with a cat's grace, padded over at her ease, and settled beside me nonchalantly, as if just nothing at all had happened. "Big John around?"

I answered her quietly, speaking as reasonably as I could, "I don't know what Big John looks like, therefore I can hardly tell if he's here—I don't even know if I'd like him if he was—*and get me out of this place right now!*"

"Stop screaming, sweetie."

"I'm not screaming!" I screamed. "But Irma—I'm so scared! I just know that they're calling the Dogcatcher."

As a matter of fact, no one was calling the Dogcatcher. Once she had made sure that Bastet was safe, Professor Frieda von Aknefrei had launched into a lecture on the importance of this particular statuette and Egyptology in general. And the cops—huge, powerful hands and chins and legs and heads, their eyes sort of glazed—were standing around, with their arms at their sides, as silent and obedient as well-behaved first graders.

(And now that I have survived—temporarily, at least—I do savor this delicious recollection! Brute strength dominated by wild intelligence! It was grand—just grand!)

"If you untie this rope with your teeth, I'll make a dash for the door!" I whispered.

"I am not unbiting any rope!" said Irma. "Just cool it now. Big John—"

"Oh, Big John!" I burst out. "He's probably just as mean and nasty as Big Hooch!" My predicament made me irrational.

"Now, how could a guy be mean and nasty who spends his

afternoons helping school kids across Hudson Street? Unless, of course, there's a guy in the adoption racket waiting on the other side."

"*Irma*—you don't think that!"

"No, of course I don't think that! Big J is the sweetest boy in New York. It was only a joke—that's all."

"Oh. A joke. Ha, ha. Yes—*ha, ha!* Irma—*help me! I'm scared!*"

Did you all know dogs could sweat? Everybody knows dogs can pant—and I was panting—but this cocker spaniel was sweating too! From the end of his nose! "You tell me to cool it, when—oh my word! Here they come!"

The officers of the Charles Street Police Station, who had just been instructed in ancient Egypt and fragile wooden statues, were now turning their attention to me. "Let's see about dis criminal dog," said the brute who had grabbed me in the alley.

"You hear that?" I murmured to Irma. "'Dis criminal dog'? Me, *Me!*—who've—rather, *I* who have sat in on lectures on Aristotle and Plato—and I prefer the latter—*rrrk!*" I *rrrk*ed because the ruffian had grabbed my collar and was choking me again.

"Looka dat. At leas' he's got a license plate. Le'see, it says, '*Hi! My name is Jerry!*'"

"Does it really say that?" leered Irma with somewhat mischievous humor. She leaned around and had a look. "Why, so it does! Hi, Jerry! Hi!"

"*Rrrr!*" Her flippancy was infuriating. I growled fiercely. That was one of my most successful growls—largely because I was being choked.

"Such a *cute* license!" Irma rubbed it in.

"I couldn't help it," I gasped to her. "All the dogs in New Haven—I mean, all the masters—wanted cute dog tags like that last year. Personally, I find it most degrading—*Rrrk!*"

"An' dere's a telephone number here." The brute let go my collar and read the telephone number out loud.

"But that's our Connecticut number!" I whined. "Oh, dear! The Thompsons forgot to change my license."

"The professor goofed, eh?"

"He doesn't goof in the classroom, Ms. Cat!" I felt obliged—and very willing—to leap to my master's defense.

"It's just Life that trips him up—right?"

"You're being singularly unpleasant!" I woofed.

While this rather disagreeable exchange took place, the sergeant was dialing the wrong number. It was answered, in a sleepy voice, by some irritated soul who spoke no English, but swore at the sergeant voluminously in what sounded to me like Polish. Although I know no Poles as yet. But this is New York and anything can happen.

A silence—a very deadly silence—followed this quick telephone call.

The sergeant shuffled some papers on his desk.

Then my arresting officer said, "Well, we can call da ASPCA—or take 'im right now to dat place ovah on Twelfth Avanoo."

An even deadlier silence ensued.

"Irma," I whispered, "what is that place on Twelfth Avenue?" She just hissed, "Shhh!"

"Where *is* Twelfth Avenue?"

"Way over on the West Side."

"Is there anything after Twelfth Avenue?"

"Not much. No. Only the river."

"*Oh*—my word!" A dog isn't supposed to faint. I kept reminding myself of that as the head inside my head began to go round and round. "If they'd only look *close*, I'm sure my license says that I'm from—"

Before I could finish—and fortunately, before any dire decision was taken—the door to the Charles Street Police Station swung open and this big, singing, hearty human being came in. There are some folk who make one trust in the world. I could see right away, this man was one.

"Thank catnip!" said Irma. "Big John! It's midnight. He's on the late shift."

Big John was a truly enormous and ruddy man, with a baritone voice with which he was roaring a happy tune. He wasn't too young, but he had attractively graying hair—the kind that drives the female human species wild. And a nice nose. Also a mustache. And honest, hazel eyes. He was very, *very* unlike the professor, but I knew right away, with our animal's intuition, that a dog—or a cat—could do no better. I sensed that he was less beastly than a lot of the human beings I've known.

He spotted Irma and halted happily in his tracks. *"My kitty!"*

"He calls you his 'kitty'?"

"Big John can call me whatever he wants!"

She raced across the concrete floor and leaped—yes, positively leaped—into his arms. That made my heart feel fragile and strange: that Irma would jump into Big John's arms.

"Hi, kitty!" Big John petted her head and kissed her. "Hi, my kitty!"

"Hi, babe," said Irma—in animal language, of course.

"Irma," I tried to remind her discreetly, "I remain tied to this sergeant's chair, and now that your *friend* has arrived, perhaps—"

"What's happenin' here?" said Big John, still fondling my cat.

He continued to tickle, tug hair, and pet her in what I thought was a most sentimental fashion, as the sergeant, the goon who'd arrested me, and, at last, Big Frieda tried to explain. It was only then that he dropped her. And high time too! I mean, dropped Irma, not Big Frieda. To the latter he tipped his hat and smiled.

Irma slipped to the floor. "It may work yet," she meowed with a matchmaker's crafty glee. "They can meet just as well in this police station—"

"A garden would be nicer."

"—as in Big Frieda's living room."

"Well, if everything else fails," I grumbled, "why don't we *all* meet at that place over on Twelfth Avanoo!"

By now there was barely contained confusion around the sergeant's desk. The goon was insisting that I was "dis criminal dog" and wondering where my criminal master was; the sergeant was asking if anything else was missing; and Frieda kept on wondering how a statue that she had remembered locking up herself could have got out the window at all.

A lull came, in which Big Frieda took the opportunity to bat her big eyes at Big John and ask him if, perchance, he was interested in Egyptology.

"Yes, ma'am," he answered dutifully, still holding his cop's hat under his arm. "On Saturday sometimes I go to the Metropolitan Museum of Art. And I like especially the Egyptian things."

"Oh, do you?" Big Frieda jumped at that. Like a contender for the Olympics, she jumped. "I know the curator. If you'd like, one Saturday afternoon we could both go up, and I'll show you some things that aren't exhibited publicly."

"He's blushing!" In a fit of anticipated success, Irma dug her claws into my shoulder. "It's going to work, Jerry baby—it is! Just look at Big John. I love to see a big guy blush!"

"Do you love to see a medium-sized cocker spaniel bleed? Because that's what *I'm* going to do—you witch's cat!—unless you unclaw my shoulder! Right now!"

She was startled by my anger, and gave me a baffled glance. "What's the matter with you? Wasn't that the whole idea? To get them together?"

"Not over *my* dead body!" I barked.

"Oh don't be such a scaredy-cat!"

"*You're* the cat!" I really was about to bite. Just grab at that lovely throat of hers and revert to all my most primitive instincts.

However, I didn't have the chance. My righteous indignation attracted Big John. He came over and knelt in front of me. "Hi, pooch!" And petted my head. "Hi, poochy-pooch."

Well let me tell you—and believe you me!—I put out all the charm I had! I waggled my little bitty tail and did all sorts of things with my eyes—the tender, pathetic glance—the *works!*

"I hope he likes you!" whispered Irma.

"I wish I looked more like a Charlie's Angel!"

"Da mutt's got a phoney license plate," said my least favorite policeman. "No one answered da call who spoke English. I t'ink we should take him right away to dat place on Twelfth Avanoo."

At last Big John stood up—all six feet six of him—and announced, "I don't want this dog to be killed."

"Lord—neither do *I!*" breathed yours truly. Dog talk, of course.

If only Irma or I—or any other intelligent animal—had just been able to talk to these people! More work really *has* to be done on this subject!

Big Frieda came and stood beside him. Big Frieda and Big John. They dwarfed all the cops in the terrible Charles Street Police Station.

"They do make a lovely couple," I said. "Especially if they save my life."

"Mmm! Changing your mind a little, I see," Irma's tail flicked my nose on its way to curling around her legs.

"We'll keep him here all night"—Big John sounded very authoritative when he was passing judgment—"and call the ASPCA tomorrow."

"Dat place on Twelfth Avanoo stays open all night."

"Oooo, Irma—I hate that man!"

"He stays right here," Big John pronounced. "Right, Sarge?"

The sergeant nodded.

"Uncurl your fur, dear," Irma purred. "It'll all be all right."

SEVEN

A Police Station— and Sad— at Night

The next six hours—from midnight until six in the morning—were the most depressing in my life. So far. But there's something I've learned in New York: things can always get worse. And they often do. But I've also learned things can always get better. Less frequently, alas.

Big John Roccasciglia—pronounced Rok-a-she-lee-ah—I made a mental note of that, for no name should be unpronounceable—said he would escort Big Frieda home. And Irma, without saying so, escorted them both home. And I was left alone, and lonely, and tied to the sergeant's desk till dawn. So I had a lot of time to rehearse Big John's last name, which I heard the sergeant address him by.

Oh, and let me tell you—a police station at night is a dreary and dull and depressing place! I hope none of you find this out for yourself! These sad, sad human beings come in. There were some who walked in, and some who staggered, and some who were dragged. The ones who walked just wanted information —like, where was the subway, or which way was New Jersey—

and they didn't worry me. The ones who staggered were usually drunk, and the cops brought them in to sober up in a special place—"the drunk tank" (ugly phrase!) it was called— or else they were sick. One man thought he had a heart attack, but admitted it might have been only gas. The cops called an ambulance to take him to Saint Vincent's, the nearest hospital, where they handle gas and heart attacks. But the ones who were dragged in—they were the worst. One had a knife—and screamed she was going to use it too! That made me *really* nervous—my word!—especially because they were holding her right beside the sergeant's desk. I licked my chops, to show I was only a dog—and kind of confused at that—and scootched behind the sergeant's chair. At last—poor soul!—she was taken away. Her name was Consuela—a lovely name! I hope she someday lives up to it.

The saddest one, though, was the man who cried. An officer led him in—quite kindly, I must say—and said that he'd found him, just sobbing away, in Abingdon Square. (That's where Hudson Street, if it goes right, bends into big Eighth Avenue.) They didn't arrest him, or put him where the drunks sober up; just sat him down, and the sergeant asked him what was wrong. No—first he asked him what his name was. Frank Ryan, said the man. Well, the sergeant's name, as I've mentioned, was Michael O'Reilly, and that seemed to cheer Frank Ryan up. They both could be Irish together, for a while. (It helps, sometimes, to be like someone else.) And *then* the sergeant asked what was wrong.

Frank said that he really didn't know; that things had just gotten to be too much. I wanted to know, *what* things? And gotten to be too much *what?* But Sergeant O'Reilly apparently knew. (And *I* may be learning.) He just nodded his head and said, yes, that things sometimes got too much for him too.

They gave Frank a paper cup of coffee—not in order to quench his thirst, I believe, but just for something to hold in his hands. And then he stopped crying, and went away with his paper cup. The sergeant wished him good luck.

Oh Frank!—Frank Ryan—where are you now? With your curly red hair and your trembly little bit of a chin. As little and

insignificant as my own little bitty tail, in fact. And have "things" gotten better? I hope they have. And I also hope that if ever *I* should find someone, either cocker spaniel or human being, who is sobbing his or her heart out in Abingdon Square, I will know what to do. But I doubt if I will. At least I will talk to anyone who might be crying in a desolate place. In fact I woofed goodbye to Frank. But I doubt he heard me.

A night of sadness, for me and for others. . . . Indeed, that was the night I began to learn how much real sadness there was in the world . . .

However, at last the reluctant dawn crept in—yes, even into that terrible and modern place. It crept around concrete corners, through windows with bars, and under steel doors. I hadn't slept a wink. But when the good sergeant, of whom I'd grown quite fond, offered me the sad end of a roast beef sandwich, I ate it—and gratefully. I wasn't hungry, but that night I learned that food is good—all food, I mean, if it's offered well—and also I didn't wish to offend.

Along with the dawn, Irma also crept in. She flickered along the walls, and no one noticed her but me. Her eyes looked tired, her whole face was haggard—as I'm sure my own was. She slumped down beside me. "Fido, this has been a night!"

"I don't especially like that name—*Irmy!*" We both were too weary to fight, however. "You haven't slept either?"

"Of course not!" She frowned at me reproachfully. "Did you think I'd just call it quits for the night? With you over here at the police station?"

"Well . . ."

What had happened, as always, was partly what everyone wanted to happen, and partly what no one expected at all. Big John, Big Frieda, Big Irma Cat, had all gone home to Frieda's apartment. And John and Frieda got nicely acquainted for a while. But then John's squad car partner burst in, saying there was some kind of emergency, and off the two cops went together to save New York from mayhem and crime.

"Then you know what the Big F did?" Irma laughed. "She got absolutely terrified!"

"I understand the feeling," I sighed.

"As soon as Big John and his sidekick had left, she thought about all those "borrowed" Egyptian artifacts, and we spent the whole night counting them, to make sure nothing else was missing. She slammed all the windows and locked them tight—the door too—and for six hours now I've been staring at chips of ancient Egyptian dishes and various other antique delights. Just fifteen minutes ago she took a sleeping pill—'to calm my nerves, kitty!': she's been talking to me like crazy too—and went to bed. But being the fresh-air fiend she is, she ventured to open one window a crack. I squinched, and pushed, and got under at last. That's one thing we've settled though, Jerry, my pet: this afternoon I am sure all the stuff goes back to the New School. Professor von Aknefrei's days as a well-intentioned thief are done! Where *is* Big John, by the way?"

"He never came back."

"Oh."

"It must have been something serious."

"Oh."

"Irma—why do you say 'oh' like that? Two times now. I have never heard you say 'oh'—I mean *'oh'*—in exactly that way before."

"Don't get worried."

But worry is something that when someone says not to do it, you *do!* "I *am* worried, Irma! I'm very worried. In fact I'm so worried that I could—"

"Simmer down." She put a paw on one front paw of mine. "Auntie Irmy will take care of her very own Jerry."

"And don't be facetious! It isn't becoming. I detest baby talk too—"

"So don't be a baby! I got you *in* this—I'll get you out."

I squelched my heart and managed to say—quite objectively —"How?"

Her tail teased the air for an answer. "There's a way out of every adventure."

That made me feel ashamed. "Irma—I mean, if it's a real adventure, you don't have to hurry, or anything. I just thought it might be—well—dangerous."

Somehow that only made matters worse. She looked at me hard, and murmured, "Dangerous," with a queer look and sound, both of which I'd never seen or heard before. "And danger we must avoid at all costs." There was sorrow, sad anger, and disbelief—just all of the things that made me feel little—in that one glance of hers.

"You kill me, Jerry," she softly said. But not the way she usually said it—as if I amazed her by being so funny and strange, and myself. I didn't feel one bit amazing just then. In fact, I didn't feel one bit myself.

"I'm really not worried, Irma," I lied.

But Irma said nothing—for a very long time.

It was courage—hers, mine, or rather, my lack of it—that curdled the air between us two.

The light grew in the Charles Street Police Station. At first I had liked it—it took away night—but now, in my Irma's disappointment in me, even daylight seemed stale.

The policemen were growing restless too. At dawn, I think— almost like nervous animals—they must always get fidgety. A new shift was coming on. But that wretch who wanted to ship me off to Twelfth Avenue was still prowling around. I think he was going to go off duty, because he kept casting me crafty glances, as if he wanted to settle my fate before he went home to bed—where the sheets, I'm sure, and everything else where he lived, could do with an airing. I don't want to be unfair, but cruelty and mouldiness are two of the things that I like least.

Irma's eyes were working now, like her tail. I could tell she was testing different possibilities. "Does Professor T have a class this morning?"

"Yes. Medieval philosophy. It begins with Saint Augustine—"

"I'm not interested in the *curriculum!* What *time* does it start?"

"At eight-thirty. It's early."

"Our first piece of luck! And maybe our last!" Her eyes flashed a look at the big round clock above the sergeant's desk. "Here's hoping, honeybunch!"

Like a streak of fall lightning turned into warm fur, she

raced from the Charles Street Police Station. The clock said quarter past eight.

I really was almost frantic then. What *was* going to happen? To pass the time, I counted my whiskers. Which I can do, if I cross my eyes. I licked my chops. They were dry as bones! And nothing could keep me from wondering what Irma was up to.

I'd gotten to six—on my whiskers, that is—when the brute made his move. "Okay—it's mornin'. Let's call Twelfth Avanoo."

The sergeant shuffled a sheaf of papers—and shuffled himself—behind his desk. "Big John said to wait—"

"Big John isn't even a sergeant, *Sarge!* He flunked da test."

"So did I. The first time."

I think that I was just beginning to understand the politics—or perhaps the psychology—of the New York Police Department, when suddenly a scream was heard. At first I thought it came from me, but actually it arose about two blocks away. I recognized the voice. Under *sane* circumstances I'd have recognized it instantly. For even screaming, Professor Thompson can sound as if some new, interesting thought had occurred.

Within seconds the two of them—Professor T and Irma (she first)—came racing into the Charles Street Police Station. "Grab it!" he roared. "Grab— [I shall omit these words.] —cat! It bit me!"

Irma's scheme—bless her feline heart!—was now as clear as the irresistible day.

"Why, Jerry—" The professor stopped short. "What are *you* doing here?"

"Woof!" I tried to explain. To no avail. That same linguistic barrier.

They arrested Irma; they set me free.

Oh, the sadness, the injustice—the *irony* of things! Is that what Frank Ryan was crying about? How nothing seems to work out right?

But at least—and at last!—I rebelled! At the sight of my dearest friend, now chained, in my place, to the sergeant's desk, my heart went wild. I snarled, I barked. My growls frightened even me. I'd almost have bitten Professor Thompson.

"Why, Jerry," he said, disbelieving, aghast, "is this you?"

"It's me!" I roared. And didn't bother to change my grammar. "You let that kitty go!" Of course no one understood.

"I want that cat tested for rabies first!" the professor said when he had collared me.

"First before what? Before what?" I demanded of her who, of all those souls, could understand me.

"Just use your imagination," said Irma. "Or rather—don't! You might *worry* too much! And find it dangerous."

They dragged her off—to Twelfth Avenue.

The professor dragged me—to freedom.

EIGHT

Mike

Need I tell you what the next day was like? Yes, I do need, in fact. I've just got to let someone know how much I suffered!

I far exceeded my previous records for fear and worry. They had to tie me down—they being the prof and Mrs. T—with a rope attached to a leg of the couch in the living room. They even called the vet—to ascertain whether I had rabies—I was acting so frantic and unlike myself. When the vet, who was rather an unimpressive young man in blue jeans, said I didn't, it occurred to the prof, with that academic mind of his, that either I had come down with a rare neurological disease or I was having a nervous breakdown. Right on *that* count! Either I had picked up some unusual germs in Greenwich Village, or else, knowing my nerves, he was sure life down here was doing me in. . . . Well, maybe he was right there too.

Poor dear human beings, they gave me hamburg meat to eat. Ground round—but I wouldn't so much as sniff at it! They changed my water every hour, and seasoned it with maple syrup, remembering my former delight in the taste. But *all* tastes—especially maple syrup, which brought back the thought of lovely baths—were bitter in my mouth.

They petted and stroked and fondled me. Every touch added

insult to injury. Except one: when the missis, in desperation, smacked my rear and told me to start behaving myself. *That* added injury to insult! I would not be consoled. Or abused! And at last they decided to let me be, having taken my temperature one last time. And oh, I was glad when *that* procedure came to an end!

I crept to the cellar, and the Thompsons knew—a whimper, a whine—that I had to be by myself. At least there, in our basement, beside our clothes dryer, I could think of . . . *her.* Alone.

Where *was* she . . . ?

Twelfth Avenue ran, straight through my brain, like the Road that runs at the End of the World. I pictured a dreadful building—barred windows and iron gates—even worse than the Charles Street Police Station. I pictured—but then I closed my eyes. And *still* the pictures wouldn't stop. Some few of us—human beings and dogs—are cursed with a really good imagination.

Oh Irma, with your tawny fur—

I decided to write a poem. "Oh Irma dear,/ Now hear me clear—" But the rhyme was revolting. As vile as one of those tuna fish sandwiches that Irma had had when she lived with the Nussters. Just *everything* made me think of her! And besides, I am a philosopher, and have little to do with anything as insubstantial as poetry.

By now it was getting on towards dinner time, on that most horrible of days, and the thought of top round ground was recurring frequently. I had just about decided to do a half hour of silent mourning, when this terrible banging abruptly shook the whole house.

At first I thought that a man from Con Edison was ripping up the sidewalk outside with one of those truly appalling jackhammers. My head was splitting as it was, but *this* was too much! I was just about to summon the master, with a long, low, doleful howl (which never fails), when at the dirty basement window I saw a blurred image—faintly yellow—alive—

"Oh, Irma!" I cried.

A voice—a very deep voice—said, "You joik! I'll mutalize ya!

Do I look like a cat?" A canary jumped in where the window was broken. And *such* a canary! My word!

"Beg pardon?" I said.

"Ya want me ta rupture dis window completely?"

"Mercy, no! Just come in. If you must."

"I bin bangin' on da sill fah minutes! Ta get yer attention."

"I thought it was a construction worker."

The canary—he isn't really big, but he gives the impression of being *huge*—hopped down from "da sill" he'd been "bangin' on." "An' youz is Jerry. Right?"

"I am."

"Oima said—"

"Irma *Cat?* Did you know the dear creature?"

"I did. An' I do. Da dear creature is now at my ol' lady's apahtment—lickin' up what's left of da milk."

"Alive!?" My heart fairly ceased to beat.

"Alive an' lickin'."

"Oh! *Oh!*"

The canary seemed somewhat amused—I might say just plain tickled, in fact—at my inarticulate joy. "If youz would like ta give her a big *'oh'* in poyson, bud, jus' follow da tail feathahs."

He hopped out over the sill, and nosing the window open, I followed him—all thought of maple syrup and hamburg meat now drowned in the swelling waves of relief.

I shan't even attempt to describe that walk downtown with Mike. For Mike was the canary's name. "Mike's da name," he said, "an' I'll poich on ya head." I'd forgotten my traveling bag, as usual, so I have to assume that any human being—police officer or dogcatcher—who saw a cocker spaniel walking down Seventh Avenue with a tough canary "poiched" on his head must just have thought he was going insane and having hallucinations. At any rate, no one bothered us. And many good folk jumped out of our way.

"I could fly much fastah," said Mike, "nat'rally, but dis way I can give youz directions."

"Oh, by all means!" I readily agreed. I would have agreed to *anything* under these circumstances.

We walked—that is, I walked, Mike rode—to a dismal area of warehouses and tenements, which was much too far downtown for my taste. And Mike told me about himself. When he had said his "ol' lady," I'd "nat'rally" taken it for granted that he was referring to some sort of a canary wife. Not a bit of it! When Mike said his "ol' lady," he did indeed mean exactly that: an agéd female human being!

"We met two years ago," said Mike, and sighed as we passed Barrow Street.

"Mike—if I might ask—implore, that is—could you loosen your grip a bit?"

"Oh. Sure. I was in dis pet shop. Don't even remembah where I was hatched. A course I coulda busted out. Evah since I was a little chick I've had dese very strong claws—"

"*Ow!* I see."

"—an' no cage could evah hol' dis canary! But one day I was swingin' dere, an' dis raggedy, doity bag lady came in—"

"What *is* a 'bag lady,' Mike? I've been referred to as one myself."

"An ol' woman which has no place to live, so she travels da city—da subways, mostly—an' lives outta shoppin' bags."

"Hmm!"

"Anyway, one day she came inta da pet shop. The ownah—a shlub, but not a bad guy—liked her an' trusted her not ta steal none of us. She loved lookin' at livin' t'ings. Boids. Fishes. Kittens an' puppies. I guess it reminded her of bein' alive—bein' young. But when she took one look at me—pow!"

"Mike!"

"Sorry. It was love at foist sight. 'You're my sweetie,' she says. I had the same feelin', but bein' a boid, all I could say to her was 'Tweet!' 'Yes, my sweetie,' she says, 'I know.' An' she did. So did I. From dat very foist day I knew us two was a pair. She ast da owner of da shop how much I was. An' him—da shlub!—he sizes da ol' woman up and says, 'Twenny-fi' cents!' Well, nat'rally she couldn't afford no twenny-fi' cents, so she looks at

me sadly an' says, 'I'm sorry, my sweetie, my dearie—I can't.' She blew me a kiss an' went out da door. Well I wasn't about ta let dat nonsense go down. I puts one claw on one of da struts of dis prison boid cage dey had me in, I puts my othah claw on da next strut ovah—an' man, did I push! I bent dat cage! Like a pretzel it looked! Den out da door—it was summah, so open— but I'da busted t'rooh anyway!—an' up da street. I caught up wit' my dahlin' an' poiched on her shouldah. She looks aroun' an' says, 'It's my sweetie!' An' I says, 'Tweet!'—meanin' 'Yup! It's me!' Since den—like, man, *inseparable!* I'm all fah her, an' she's fah me!"

"Mike," I ventured to interrupt, "this is really very interesting, but, well, this neighborhood—"

We had gone down Seventh Avenue and made a right, and then a left—I forget how many turns there were—and the whole city seemed to have gone to the dogs. An expression, by the bye, that has always seemed to me needlessly offensive.

"These blocks look like—if I *must* say it—slums."

"So whaddaya expect for a shoppin' bag lady an' her canary? Da Waldorf?"

Right then I made up my mind that *this* canary should not be questioned, except on the most important occasions. We passed by derelict tenements and vacant lots, garbage in the streets—I didn't so much as woof my distaste.

On one especially distressing corner some human bums had made a fire in a big oil drum. They were drinking too— straight out of the bottle—and it wasn't lemonade or Perrier water.

"Looka dose poor guys," Mike said with a softness I hadn't heard from him before.

"They're drunk!" I exclaimed. And forgetting momentarily my resolve of last night, I stepped off the sidewalk, avoiding them.

"So what if dey're fried outta shape?" said Mike. "Dey got nuttin' in life. Dey're makin' it be less painful, dat's all. Poor guys. A lotta people get fried outta shape." His claws gripped more firmly. "Youz is some kinda snob, ain't ya?"

"I try not to be. Ouch! *Please!* I reformed last night."

"Well okay, furry-face, as Oima calls ya—but remember dis: dere are times in life, fah joy or fah sorrow, when a guy has *got* ta get fried outta shape."

"I'll remember, Mike."

"Hi, you guys!" he shouted at the bums. I guess it just sounded like "tweet" to them—but being drunk, or "fried outta shape," as my friend would have it—perhaps they understood. I managed an amicable "woof" myself.

"An' don't knock da neighbahood! It took me weeks ta find a pad fah me an' my ol' woman," said Mike. "Da foist t'ing I knew I had ta do, aftah we'z two got in touch, was to find a decent place fah her. No subways, no pahks, no sleepin' on benches— not fah dis canary's lady! I trained her foist ta sit down, just sit by peckin' her on da shouldah twice't. An' aftah dat foist night, which we spent in Cent'ral Pahk, I decided dat we'z two needed a pad. So I sat her down in Cent'ral Pahk an' went out lookin'. I foun' da apahtment where we live now. Da buildin' had been desoited—"

"We're going to an *abandoned* building?"

"You bet! An' a foist-class, run-down dump it is! Da people even left some cans in da cupboard. We've had food fah mont's! I really lucked in when I foun' dis dump. So back I flew to Cent'ral Pahk, an' directed my ol' lady by pecks—lef', right— down here to da watahfront. An' here we are, as a matta of fact!"

We were, indeed, on the waterfront. My word! I never thought I'd sink so low. But it *wasn't* so low, come to think of it.

I had stopped because Mike squeezed my scalp, in front of a three-storey brick ruin. To me it suggested nothing but fleas— and you can guess my abhorrence for *them!*—but to Mike, I guess it felt like home. I sighed with relief as he hopped off my head.

"Two flights up, my cockerel spaniel frien'!"

"*Cocker* spaniel," I corrected him, as we entered the dismal place.

Dust—soot—old plaster falling down. I knew my coat would

be a mess. Cracked walls—and ceilings that weren't even *there!* But dogfully I followed him. Up two flights of stairs. No bannisters—you could break your neck.

But there, on floor three, at a door half off its hinges, was Irma Cat!

The human beings, overcome by emotion, rush into one another's arms. We animals just rush. And bump.

"Hi, babe!"

"You're safe! Oh, Irmy—" I controlled myself.

In the gladness of being together again, we told each other what we'd done in the meantime. The best meantimes—for me at least—are those that happen between seeing a friend. But Irma's story was much more exciting than mine. That hooligan Hooch cop had tied her feet, since he rightly mistrusted my Irma's claws, and tossed her on the floor of his squad car, Then off they roared to that most unspeakable place on Twelfth Avenue.

"I don't want to hear about it!" said I. Because Irma, knowing how nervous I got, *had* got, and always *will* get, was about to launch into a long and detailed description.

"It's made of black slate—"

"Irma—stop!"

"—and a soulless, ghostly concrete!" She smiled with beguiling mischief.

But I'll let you in on a secret now. We cocker spaniels have very long ears—very heavy ears too. And there is a way—which I am forbidden to tell, and very few humans know this—that we can clamp our ears tight shut! And you can believe that I shut my ears now. It just took one sentence—"This guy who was there had black leather gloves!"—for me to blot out all the rest. But then, through the battened-down skin of my ears, I heard her say "Big John," so I unblocked and listened awhile.

The Big J, it seems, had come back to the Charles Street Police Station, after keeping two people from killing each other, and on hearing that his favorite kitty was fast approaching oblivion, he too had dashed off to Twelfth Avenue. (I don't know *what* the neighbors thought, with all those cop cars

screaming up.) And at the last moment—the *very* last moment!—Big John had plucked Irma to safety, right out of a
hand that was gloved in black leather. Then Big John had
taken Irma home. To *his* home, that is. With his own iron
weights, and his mother's china.

"But I only stayed a few hours," sighed Irma. "It's gone too far
between us already. Of course he knows I love him—"

"You *love* him!"

"Sure. And he loves me. A great big gorgeous cop like that—
how could a kittycat not love Big John?"

"*Really,* Irma!"

"He let me go, though. Without too much of a scene, I mean.
He knows I'll be back—when I want to, that is."

I wouldn't give her the satisfaction of showing her how
distressed—how destroyed—I felt. I did fidget, though; this I
have to admit. "Well, since things are going so—lovingly—"
There was bitterness in my voice. I know there was: I put it
there! "I'm surprised that you sent Mike Canary here to
summon me all the way to the slums."

"I knew you'd be worried—"

"Oh! I wasn't," I lied, as airily as I could. "The missis gave me
an extra Milk Bone, and I had a little nap—that's all."

Would I tell her of my anguish? No! . . . Would I tell her I'd
almost written a *poem?* I would *not!*

"Mmm," meowed Irma. I hope she believed me. (But I still
don't know.)

"Dese are not da slums, furry-face!" said Mike Canary, who'd
been listening to us with as much amusement as has ever
been shown in a streetwise canary's face. "Dis is me an' my ol'
lady's home!" He got all eager. "Ya wanna see her?"

"I should be delighted!" said I, as delightedly as I could. "A
pleasure to meet someone civilized!" I jabbed Irma with a
glance. At least tried.

"I dunno 'bout bein' civilized—"

He hopped ahead of us down a hall where at least the dirt
was dry and neat, all pushed to one side by Mike himself. In
fact I would say that the dirt in Mike's and his ol' lady's

apartment was as clean as dirt can ever be. One had the impression of poverty, but also—well it was as I'd said just moments ago, but hadn't meant: one had the impression of Civilization. Just people and animals being nice. And thinking of one another's wants. With a little good talk.

That day I got to like Mike Canary—and Irma Cat—and even myself—quite a lot. . . . Even more than I'd liked us before.

NINE

~

Mike's Ol' Lady

"Dere she is!" In what passed for a kitchen—a sink, a stove—Mike gestured upwards with his right wing. "Ain't she *great*?"

In a rocking chair, beside the stove, sat this very *old* ol' woman. Her dress was gray, and so was her hair. Her eyes were gray too. Every single thing about Mike's ol' lady was some shade of gray. Or lavender, if the light was right.

Mike flew up to her shoulder, leaned over, and stupidly I thought for a moment that he meant to peck her. He only just barely touched his bill to her cheek. She looked at him, and seemed to see nothing. Then the light of a smile dawned over her face. She'd recognized her friend. "Hi, my sweetie!"

"Tweet! Tweet!" was what the old woman heard. But Irma and I heard Mike say, "Hi, hon'!"

The cat and I, who had now quite forgotten our own petty spat, looked at each other, to share in Mike's love.

"I moved her inta da kitchen las' wintah. Da buildin's abandoned, but da guys from Con Ed forgot to cut da gas. So dere's warmth from da stove. But den, come spring, I couldn't get her outta here. She just t'inks dat dat rockin' chair, right nex' ta da stove, is where she lives."

"What's wrong with that?" said Irma. "She's happy."

"*Eggzackly!*" said Mike. "Da only t'ing is—I worry about da gas."

Along the stove, just below the handles to turn on the gas—it really was very old, that stove—ran a porcelain pipe. Mike hopped along that porcelain pipe, and at every handle he pushed with his shoulder—if canaries have shoulders—he pushed where his wing joined his husky yellow body, to make sure that the gas was off. "Dese stick sometimes. *Rrrff!*"

"What a canary!" said Irma Cat, dazed with unfeline admiration.

I agreed, but said nothing. Unusual for me—but I still was thinking.

"I'll be wit' youz two in a minute."

While Mike went on down the pipe, I asked Irma, "Is it safe here, though—really? For old ladies and even the toughest canaries?"

Irma shrugged. "As safe as New York can be. And I pity the burglar who breaks in here."

"I suppose Mike'd fight dirty—like peck at eyes—to protect the old lady."

"He wouldn't need to!" Irma laughed. "With one wing he could knock any burglar unconscious."

"Oima," said Mike, "while I was off fetchin' da pooch, did da ol' woman—" He hopped: a short jump of embarrassment, on the porcelain pipe. "Did she, like, do what she'd oughtta do?"

"Yes, Mikey," nodded Irma, "I guided her there and back again. Everything is fine."

Mike seemed relieved. "Den dinnah time!" He flew up to a cupboard above the somewhat untidy sink, took hold of the handles, and, beating backwards with his wings, pulled open the doors. And vanished inside.

"He's amazing!" I said. "Irma, where did you meet him?"

"I'll tell you later," whispered the cat. "Just listen, look—and learn."

Inside the cupboard we could hear Mike Canary tumbling things, which sounded like cans, all around. His head popped out; he flew down to the old woman's shoulder. "We got tuna fish, we got deviled ham. An' we also got dog food. But not fah youz, Jerome! I'm savin' da not-nice stuff fah her when ev'yt'ing else is gone. So how's about it, dahlin'? Tuna fish?"

She waved her hand vaguely in his direction. But what she *saw*—who, who knows that? "It's my sweetie! Hi, sweetie!" she said.

Mike shook his head. There was sadness and laughter in his face. You would be astounded at how much emotion there is to be shown in the tiny eyes of a little bird! "She still t'inks we're back in da pet shop," said Mike. "Well—tuna fish it is!" He flew to the cupboard.

Irma and I said not a word. Since we had the same thoughts, what need to speak?

But at last I had to say, "Big Frieda and Big John. You call everybody in New York *'big.'* But Irma—he's the one. He may just look like a yellow little fuzzy puffball—but Irma, that guy is *Big* Mike!"

She glanced at me with a smile that came from way inside. Then, to spare us both from getting too close, she flicked my nose with the tip of her tail. "There's hope, there is. Some *do* grow up! My word—some really do."

At this critical juncture of understanding, a can of tuna fish came rolling out of the cupboard and landed—*bang!*—on the sink. Mike's head poked out. "Dere's on'y two tuna fishes left. An' one ham. An' a coupla cans dat I don't undahstan'. We'll be eatin' dog food by Chris'mas. Nuts!"

"We'll help you!" said I, standing up, to help—and also to stop my heart from hurting.

"Help wit' what?"

"Why, to open that can. You can't—"

Irma and Mike both laughed together. And before I could say "Aristotle" or "Plato," Mr. Big Mike Canary had started to *peck* that tin can open.

"Irma!" I said. "He'll break his bill!"

"Oh, no I won't!" Mike had gone halfway round. "I done dis before." He finished the top of the can—*rat!-tat!-tat!*—and flipped it open.

I only could gasp. "I wouldn't have thought an eagle could do that!"

"No eagle could," Ms. Cat explained.

"Now youz two can help. Dis can is heavy—"

Without another word on Mike's part, we had jumped to the sink and lifted the can of tuna fish, with tooth and claw—my teeth, her claws—to the stove, next to which the old lady was sitting. Mike flew back to the cupboard. More rumbling—but tinnier sounding now. He flew out with a spoon clasped in his bill.

"Oh, really, Mike," I said, "this won't do! Even here—and I'm not even sure where 'here' is—we at least can eat off clean utensils." I took the spoon, pushed on the water, and washed it thoroughly. Now I have to admit that I did this for two reasons: one, I *do* like cleanliness; and two, I suddenly felt a need to be part of the life that Mike and his old lady were leading there in that nondescript slum.

"Okay, Jerome!" Mike chuckled—if a canary can chuckle. Believe me, they can! "Dat spoon is sterilized by now. But dis is da hahd paht." He seized the spoon in his two claws and flew it to the old woman's hand. She dropped it immediately. "Youz see? I can't *feed* her!" Poor wingéd soul! He felt it as failure. But I did not.

"Can we—"

"I could—"

"No, no. Youz can't. On'y *I* can! Youz can lif' da can ovah on da stove a little nearer—if youz please."

We did as instructed.

"Now dis may take a while." Again—and again—and then over and over—he put that spoon in the woman's hand. At last her fingers closed, like old roots, and held it fast. Mike flew her hand, now holding the spoon, to the can. Something fell into shape in her mind. She began, like a human machine, to eat. Up-down, up-down, went her hand: she *ate!* . . . And we three animals breathed a sigh of triumph, together.

Mike sat on the stove. He's the only canary that I have known who could sit, with his little feet stretching out, on his rump.

And he was exhausted. "Whee-oo! Dat's da hahdest part. But once she stahts, it's okay."

"Do you do this every day?" I asked.

"It's easier. Sometimes."

"I met Mike"—Irma dashed in, with cheery information, to make it easier for us right then—"last March! I had just abandoned the somewhat dreary domestic charms of Nussterville, when I nearly got eaten alive by a mastiff."

"My word!"

"Yeah! An' Oima's evah-lovin' life!" Mike remembered the incident very well.

"I may say"—Cat flashed her tail—"it was indeed a memorable experience. I almost felt homesick for the Nussters—and the boob tube too. I was on a real downer—and just then there appeared the biggest [swearword] dog you ever saw! And he must have come from some primitive suburb, because, being big and huge and a mutt, he felt obliged to pick on the nearest kittycat. I'd about decided the jig was up—all nine lives shot at once—when out of the blue zoomed Mike Canary and landed on that hairy dinosaur's skull. I think that the brute was shocked, more than anything else—to be attacked by this tiny collection of yellow feathers."

"'Shocked,' my tiny yellow tail feaddahs!" said Mike. "When dis boid pecks, he *pecks!* I'da drilled a hole in his head—da bum! I'da mutalized him!" He laughed chirpily. "But den I t'ought Oima might go aftah me. Youz know—da ol' nonsense: dogs chase cats, an' cats chase boids, and boids chase woims— *Yecch!* Not fah me."

"Me neither, sweetie!" said Irma. "This is one cat who lives by live-and-let-live. Cats, birds—*and* woims!"

"Escuse me, please. We got a little problem here."

Mike, who had joined us two on the floor, had been keeping one beady black eye on the old woman, eating. Now a dog, I know—your usual dog—has no right to criticize table manners, but alas, the lady had spilled quite a lot. Mike fluttered and perched, and perched and fluttered, and picked up bits of tuna fish in his bill. The bits that he thought might still be clean—and his judgment was fairly generous—he dropped back into the can for her to eat, but the dirty scraps, from the floor or the arms of her rocking chair, he flew to the sink. A push with one wing turned on the faucet, and it was by little chores like this that he kept the kitchen as clean as it was.

"Dere, now!" He picked one final speck from her chin—it surely was sanitary enough—and popped it into her mouth for her. Then he blinked his eyes down at Irma and me, and said for himself and his ol' lady, "We done real good tonight!" . . . Indeed . . . oh, indeed!

"So since that mastiff got his comeuppance, Mike C and I have been good buddies," said Irma. "I thought I had better come down here and avoid your cellar, until that nip I gave the professor heals."

I was so fascinated by watching the way Mike Canary took care of his lady in public—so attentive and private—yes, private in public—I barely could focus on Irma at all. "Oh, yes. Yes, sure. I'm sure that Professor T won't miss you. And anyway—this way I got to meet Mike."

"Now, da suppah bein' done—we sing! Okay, Big Jer?"

Beneath my fur I did blush then, from thanks as well as embarrassment. Someone called me *"Big"* Jer!

"We sing?"

"We sing!" Irma's tail lightly flicked my whiskers and ended the questioning.

"Ya know," Mikey—I mean, *Big* Mikey—explained, "Ol' human bein's have trouble sleepin'."

"Oh, so do some old dogs I know!" My effort to help—to lend gentleness and a life lived in common to both old dogs and old human beings—was not in the slightest necessary. Mike knows by instinct so *much* that I have to learn by thought.

"An' usually I sing alone. But youz guys bein' here"—his black eyes twinkled—"we t'ree all can sing!"

"Mike," I apologized, "I'm afraid I *can't* sing!"

"Nat'rally. But youz can loin!"

I sighed, defeated—"Nat'rally!"—but happily, gladly defeated too. I would try to sing.

Also, the time of the day—and the year—were a help. It was golden October, the cool gold of a clear late afternoon. And by some miracle of destruction, the buildings around the old lady's house had all been torn down in precisely the right way: we saw the river! The Hudson River. For a few weeks, or maybe, if lucky, months, she had a view of the huge and quiet stream that seems to drain away all the hurry and scurry, the harming and hurting, of New York. Whiskers knows how long her own building will last—but it lasted long enough that day. . . . It lasted so long that from that afternoon on, I'll always compare my happiness to it.

"We staht wit' 'My Buddy,'" said Mike.

"Oh dear—"

"Don't worry, hon'." Irma patted me with a paw. And she hadn't done that before. Just snapped her tail at me. "If you don't know the words, just hum along."

Which I did. The words, as I remember them, were "Buddy! My buddy! Nobody's buddy but mine!" Or some such doggerel. Another word that—oh well, no matter.

I howled the tune, and Irma meowed, and Mike chirp-chirped. And Heaven knows what the neighbors thought! If there even were neighbors, in such a place.

That canary, though! I say chirp-chirped, but actually he sounded much more like a big and husky young human man—with hair on his chest!—who was singing in the bathtub. My word! When he sang "My buddy!"—well, some-body—the ol' woman, I guess—really was his pal.

The second song was a solo for Mike. Ms. Irma Cat insisted on that. "I know 'Sweethearts,'" she said. "And nobody sings it like Mike. It's from an old movie, *Maytime*. The Nussters' favorite. They stayed up till dawn to see it sometimes. So did I. They cried and they cried over 'Maytime.'"

"Yes," I said. "The Thompsons love it too."

"But nobody—I mean, *nobody*—sings 'Sweethearts' like Mike. So sing—you bullfinch, nightingale, canary, you!"

Mike settled on the old woman's shoulder. He folded one wing across his chest. "Sweethot . . . sweethot . . . sweethot . . . will you . . . love me . . . evah?"

I can't remember all the words. I don't need to remember all the words. I shall never forget the deep feeling that lay beneath all those musical-comedy words.

That song, for some deep reason, seemed to bring the old lady back into herself. She muttered, "Frank!" And then suddenly, she knew who she was, where she was. She looked at Mike, and in her own voice—not the vague sounds she'd been making till now—she said, "Thank you, dear. I had almost forgotten."

Then her age came again: her hand waved—her eyes glazed—and she stared at nothing, at everything.

The last song, at Mike's insistence, was "Fah she's a jolly good fellow." Even I knew the words to that, and sang it lustily. The old lady, wherever she might be, enjoyed it very much herself. She rocked back and forth with great enthusiasm, and laughed! How she laughed! And all in the past . . .

"Easy, sweet," Mike warned. "Ya'll rock yaself right out da window."

With a few nods of her head—up, down—as if she agreed with herself somewhere—a little shuffling in the rocking chair—the old woman started to fall asleep.

"It took less time dan usual," said Mike. "Youz t'ink she needs a blanket, Oima?"

"You have *blankets?* I disbelieved, for a moment. "That you can lift?"

"Puppy dog, in da uddah room dere are blankets dat I can lift! I on'y wish dey was Poishan cahpets." He glanced out the window. The world had grown brilliant—an autumn clarity—but chill, in the setting sun. The outlines of buildings stood vivid and sharp, like a pencil scrawl across the light. "It's gettin' on wintah." He heaved a sigh that might have come from an eagle. "Oh, well—we just gotta take it as it comes."

Mike did one last thing, before letting the old lady fall into sleep. With his bill he tried to comb her hair. I think it may have embarrassed him to be seen with his bill combing down and down, and smoothing over that raggedy hair, because he stopped and muttered. "Fah niceness, ya know. Dat's all."

My heart felt so queer and fragile again that I didn't dare

even to look at Irma. If it wasn't Big John and Jealousy, it was Big Mike and the Sorrow of Things. Two hurts in my heart in one day: one good—which is love—and one not so good— which is selfishness. Oh, well . . .

Mike flew down to the floor, now mindful of us, his duty done. "Hey! Youz two hungry? She ate up one can of tuna fish, but dere must be somet'in' else left."

"Oh, please!" I said. "You'll need all the food you can get!"

"Da heck wit' dat! Youz two is guests. An' me an' she doesn' have dem too often." His yellow wings whirred—he was up in the cupboard. "Le's have a pahty! Right?"

"Right!" said Irma, and silenced me—she seems to be always silencing me—with the merest understanding glance.

"Oh, by all means!" I agreed heartily—as usual to I-didn't-know-what. A "pahty"? What kind of a "pahty"?

Mike rummaged in the cupboard. We heard cans tumbling, and occasionally a swearword from Mike as something dropped on him in the darkness. "More tuna fish. Nope—we can't have dat. Or canned peas, or canned corn. All da t'ings da ol' lady can eat I save like di'munts!"

"Mike," I called up. "We really don't need to eat anything. We'll have a party by *knowing* we're having a party, that's all."

"Da heck wit' dat!" his voice came out. "Do youz two t'ink dat me an' my ol' lady ah bums?" More rumbling, tumbling, bumbling. And then a grumbling silence. "Hey, youz guys— what's babies in rum?"

Irma and I, confidants though we are, could only stare at each other aghast. We had shared much together—but pickled *children*?

"Anyway—here she comes!" Mike rolled out a can, which crashed in the sink. And instantly my cat and I leaped up there to examine it.

"It isn't babies," Irma sighed with relief.

"It's baba-au-rhum," I explained. "A delicious French dessert. The professor and Mrs. T had it often in New Haven. Especially when the prof had need to impress the head of his department at Yale. I recognize this can, in fact. An *excellent* brand, and—"

"Would it nouritch da ol' lady?"

"I don't really know. But I doubt it, Mike. The dessert contains liquor."

"*Booze?*"

"Well, yes. That's the rum. But—"

"*Stan' back!*"

I really feared for Mike's bill then. He went after that can like a bank robber after an iron safe. *Tat-tat-tat!* And then he took a breath. "An' ol' lady should *nevah* have dis!" *Tat-tat-tat.* He pried the lid open . . . and I must admit, a delicious fragrance filled the air.

Mike took to his wings and hovered above the now open can. "Oh wow! Oh wow!"

"Irma," I whispered, "I think one of us should warn the canary. The rum that they use can be *very* strong—"

"Will you just shut up?" Irma thrust her face, which really wasn't all that angry, right up to mine. "Will you let us just enjoy ourselves? And enjoy yourself too! If it isn't too late!"

At that very second—because of Irma's flashing eyes and Mike's lovely hover above the open baba can—I made up my mind that Philosophy should be left at home. Or at school. Or out in the streets. At least that it shouldn't interfere with a party held in a tenement. I decided not to philosophize: I wouldn't think. For a while, I'd just feel!

"Who gets da foist?"

"You, Mike!" "Oh you!" said Irma and I, in chorus.

Mike gulped up a baba. The babas are scrumptious lumps of pastry. The rhum is rum, which they're swimming in. A delectable sight, they are, I might add! A delectable taste too. "Oh man! Oh wow!"

My baba made me choke. But Irma's just made her say "*Mmm!*" in an altogether new tone of voice. While Irma and I were savoring ours, Mike kept on downing one after another.

"One of us must warn him, Irma," said I, with a giggle, "about the strength of rum."

"Well *this* one won't!" She licked her whiskers.

"Nor will I!" And *I* licked my *chops!* Not reflectively, but just because my chops were *mine!* And also they tasted good.

"I gotta have anothah baba!" said Mike. "I'm gettin' fried outta shape!"

"Irmy—" My eyes closed in on her, sort of. "In Mike's own language, 'fried outta shape' means—tipsy. If not downright drunk."

"Well, *let* him!" she growled, becoming tigerlike. Which I found both appealing and threatening. "Just look what he has to take care of! *Look!*"

In her rocking chair, asleep, the old lady was tipping back and forth. Her hair, which Mike had so carefully combed, had tangled itself all up again. And—something that really upset me a lot—a little trail of spit was dribbling down her chin.

"Youz want anothah baba?" Mike called to me.

"Nat'rally!"

We all had babas. And then more babas. We had—oh, delicious!—babas galore.

"An' now we sing!" Mike teetered back and forth on the edge of the baba can.

"We already shang." My intelligence never fails me. "An' beshides, she'sh ashleep."

"So we sing for ourselves." Irma Cat was dancing—and in slow motion—all around the kitchen floor. "I'll start."

She sang—and this disturbed me at first—"Three Blind Mice." I thought that she might be reverting. But no. She sang about those three blind mice—poor souls; the carving knife—as if they'd been her dearest friends. And—knowing Irma—they probably were. Poor darlings! I was feeling sentimental too. If ever I should meet three blind mice, I'll always help them across the street.

Then *I* was forced to sing. A baba helped, but I still had trouble and felt a great deal of embarrassment. Yet I did get through "The Battle Hymn of the Republic." . . . "Trampling out the vintage where the grapes of wrath are stored!" . . . A mighty song is that! But I hiccupped once, and almost ruined the grand effect.

And then it was Big Mikey's turn. His being a canary, I thought he'd warble something lyric. Not a bit of it! He flew to the windowsill—and crashed on it—and, looking at the big

Hudson River, sang "Ol' Man River" and then, as a kind of drunken dividend, "Deep River" too.

I tell you it was something to *cry* over! Which we three did. It was all so real! And loving. An' lovely. An' we were friends. Forever, we were! . . . Nat'rally!

And we had the last babas.

Irma made me put my head in the sink. Then she ran cold water over me.

"I'm fried outta shape!" said Mike, at peace. He was lying on top of the sink. One little thin leg was sticking over the edge. It seemed so helpless. And yet Mike was so strong.

"Will he be all right?"

"Of course," said Irma.

She walked me to the door. And then said, "But will you? You've forgotten your bag."

"The [swearword] with my bag!"

"Oh. Mmm," she purred. "I see we've become a salty dog."

"I'm not salty, Irma," I explained. "It's just that I don't need my bag all the time!" I fidgeted. "I'll get home all right." And I fidgeted even more. Unspoken things give me the fidgets. "You'll watch out for Mike? You'll go down the stove, and make sure all the gas faucets are off?"

"I will," said Irma, "I'll do everything. You worry too much."

"I'm sorry, Irma," I tried to explain, "but drunken canaries do worry me!"

Then Irma did something. She always does something that worries me! She kissed me right on the tip of my nose. I was absolutely flabbergasted! . . . And then she batted me—with one paw, exactly where she had kissed me before. "Go home," she said. "You worry too much." With a casual paw-push she shut the door.

And so, without my bag, I went home . . . through dark, dangerous streets. . . . And I thought about Irma and Big Mike . . . and Big John and Big Frieda too . . . and the missis and the prof. . . .

I thought about *Life!* . . . A very big thing. Which I still didn't understand too well, when I finally got home.

But I did make it home.

TEN

Brenda Blan-*deen* (and Edgar Too)

"Oima's in da window!"

With such a pecking and pounding and pummeling on the windowsill, it could only be one soul I know. "Hi, Mike! How's the old lady?"

"She's okay. But ya gotta come right now. Because Oima's—"

"I really enjoyed that evening, Mike. And I've been thinking: I just happen to know where the missis stores her canned goods—"

"Yeah, but—"

"—and although, ordinarily, pilfering is a thought that would perish instantly from my mind—"

"Yeah, but—"

"—since your ol' lady's such a really darling senior citizen, I think now and then I can help you out with tuna fish and deviled ham and a variety of canned vegetables." I was rather pleased with this offer, in fact. It had been several days since I'd been down to Mike's, and I'd stored up my generosity and the kindly feelings that came therefrom. "There might even be," I hinted discreetly, "a few tasty and invigorating desserts!"

"You *joik!*" Mike stamped angrily on the windowsill: a feathered fury. "I'm tellin' youz, *Oima's in da window!* Now get ya furry butt outta here, before I staht drillin' a hole in ya head!"

"We'll, if you put it that way—"

I upped and outed into the yard. Mike wouldn't even ride on my head. He was in such a tizzy—no, really a frenzy—of mad impatience, and dashed through the air ahead of me with such impetuosity that I thought he really might fracture my skull if I delayed. But then I remembered suddenly, and went back for my bag. "Oh youz floppy-eared, sad-eyed, mutton-headed joik!" He trod the empty space, just like a humming-bird, and waited, in desperation, for me.

"What window, Mike?"

"Ya'll see! Ya'll see!"

We threaded our way through the winding streets of Greenwich Village, and turned left on Greenwich Avenue. It was a lovely and purple evening. For even in cities, there are certain evenings both sweet and sharp, especially in autumn: the air grows chill—the light magically bright—and one's coat feels really so comfortable! A rich twilight, thickening into night, seemed to hug all the human beings so close—us animals too—and even the tawdry electric signs all looked like lamps, enchanted and wonderful, that were shining down on all things good.

We stopped before a very large meadow: a vast pane of glass in front of a showroom. Behind it were couches, chairs, footstools, beds—and all beautifully upholstered too. It was one of the very finest furniture stores in all the Village. Indeed, in my humble but well-informed opinion, it could easily compete with the shops on Fifth Avenue.

I was letting my eyes graze over the fabrics and elegant shapes—a deep-wine-colored easy chair was absolutely fabulous—when suddenly I saw a tail. A familiar tail, drooping over the edge of a beige chaise longue. It winked at me! "My word! That's Irma!"

"Yeah!" Mike squeaked. "I been tellin' youz!" Like a lot of big guys—big in one way, but tiny and nice in another—he had a high, raspy laugh that was little and funny and lovely to hear.

Irma flicked her tail at me again—in a most flirtatious way, I thought—and then jabbed towards the back of the store with it.

"Come roun' to da back. We can get in dere."

O my New York! You metropolis of skyscrapers and enormous highways! If it weren't for your byways and private alleys, you wouldn't be yourself at all. You wouldn't be cozy, as well as huge.

We zigged and we zagged behind two buildings, jumped up on an ash can—at least I jumped—and Mike gestured with one wing at a window. "Now push dat glass wit' ya buttony little nose!" I did, and it swung in. "It's easiah when da windows swing in," said Mike.

"Yes indeed!" I agreed. By now I'd had so much experience in breaking into stores, homes, and apartments, I was feeling like your regular New York burglar. "Nat'rally! The swing window is easiah!"

"Ah youz makin' *fun?*"

"No. Perish the thought! And bury it too! Lead on, Big Mike."

We made our way through the cluttered back room of the store. There was furniture piled everywhere, not as nicely displayed as the pieces that could be seen from the street. But excellent merchandise, I could see. Then quietly we crept up behind the chaise longue where Irma was lying.

"You there?" she asked, having heard our tippy-toe approach.

"We are," I whispered. "What are you doing here?"

"Stay out of sight!" I caught a glimpse of a languid paw lying over a cushion. "I'm modeling."

"You're *modeling?*"

"Will you please keep quiet! You're barking like Lassie."

Another of Irma's adventures, it seems. She explained what had happened, sort of speaking backwards, if you see what I mean, to where Mike and I crouched behind the chaise longue. "Two days ago I just happened to be strolling down Greenwich Avenue, and I passed this boutique—"

"A boutique?" I asked. Although I hate to admit that I don't know what everything means.

"Furry-face," she explained, "in New York a boutique is a store that costs a lot."

"Pray go on."

"And in *this* very window, on *this* very chaise longue, I saw this really beautiful girl. She was modeling the furniture. You know, lounging around on everything so the passersby could see how attractive all these overpriced items are. Well I stopped, and I just had to purr. She's so pretty, Brenda is! Not at all made up or full of lipstick and rouge and junk. She's just plain beautiful! Brenda Blan-*deen.* That's the way she is forced to pronounce it, for fashion's sake, although it's spelled B-l-a-n-d-i-n. Anyway, she saw me pause and purr—couldn't hear, of course, I was on the outside—but she waved so sweetly I said to myself, 'That's one human being I've got to know!' I creepy-crept in, and located her here, and jumped into her lap—and Jerry, we two have become like sisters."

"A curious family," I couldn't prevent myself from commenting.

"No lip now, bud!" Irma thrashed her tail. "You'll like her too. Or else! And Edgar too."

"Who is Edgar?"

"Just wait. So Brenda and I were playing together—and what do you know? We attracted a crowd! A *much* bigger crowd than when Brenda was lounging alone. It was—you know—a beautiful girl and a—well, a—"

"A knockout cat!" said Mike gallantly. I had felt the same sentiment, but chose not to speak.

"It was something that hadn't been seen before. Not in this store, anyway. New! *New!* That's all the humans care about. So we were a team. The owner, a rather unsavory character named Rodney Sturder, said I could stay. Good business, of course. The hypocritical wretch! And anything to keep Brenda happy. And Brenda is overjoyed, because I can keep her company. We do our tricks—play, kid around—she strokes my hair—and the folks jam their noses against the glass. Edgar loves me too."

"Now who *is* Edgar?"

"He's Brenda's boyfriend. And also the stock boy in this store. And also a student of certified public accounting in night school. He hustles the furniture only to pay for his studies."

"So what is a Soitified public accountance?" Mike asked.

"I don't know exactly," Irma said, "but it's business and it's economy, and it's a good living."

"I believe I can explain," I offered.

"Please don't," said Irma. "We'll be here for the rest of the winter. And Brenda's in school too."

"Majoring in cosmetics?" I woofed wittily.

"She is *learning* to take dictation and type!"

"The beautiful girl you say she is, and she wants to be—"

"A secretary! Yes, you male chauvinist canine pig! She models only to make the money to go to school—and help Edgar too, since he earns much less. She doesn't actually have the—how can I put it?" Irma's tail put it very elegantly. "The *calling* for modeling that I do myself. But she does very well, for an amateur. The only thing is—she falls asleep. From studying so much." With utmost discretion, my cat glanced away. "Books don't come easily to the girl."

"Dumb, huh?" Mike Canary said that! Not I!

"Now listen, my little feathered friend! You too can be eaten, if I should decide to revert to type. They both do their best, and I'm mad about them! So human, somehow. But when Brenda begins to fall asleep, that's where I come in. I purr, I meow, I lightly bat her with a paw." With a shrug of her whiskers Irma unhid the truth. "Once yesterday I even had to howl like a banshee to get the sleepy goddess awake. But I did it! I've made up my mind to stay on this job until they both have graduated —and please, Bastet, don't make it too long!—and can move to Ohio."

"O-*hi*-o!"

"Will you catch a load of him?" Irma asked Mike. "Three months in New York and already a snob. Yes, my supersophisticated, stubby-tailed friend, Brenda and Edgar want to live in Ohio. Her folks are from Akron, and people are happy there too."

"My word!" I shook my head. "The things one does learn."

Irma's head clicked into the listening position. "Here they come! They've been out on a break." She jumped down. "Come on. Let's watch them together." Her tail did a little wink in the air. "It's so cute."

"It's immoral!" said I. "It's eavesdropping. Where should we hide?"

"Behind that orange sofa. Quick!"

"I don't like orange, Irma."

"Will you get out of sight! Mike—*peck* him!"

I got out of sight. Quite rapidly. At this point in time I'd acquired a healthy respect for Mike's bill, little though it might be.

The two human beings—Brenda Blan-*deen* and Edgar (his last name was Veasy, by the bye)—made their way amid all the furniture, holding hands.

Now of course I know more about dogs, and spaniels especially, but that Brenda was something wonderful! She had auburn hair, blue eyes, and rose petal lips. She was slender as a willow wand. And her arms and legs, and all of her, just seemed to be doing a dance all the time! Her movements were like ballet. If you know what that is. And I do. The professor sometimes discusses "the dance of ideas" in his class.

But Edgar—ye gods! He was short and skinny, and had scraggly hair. One eye went in its own direction. And his *clothes!* I would not dare say this out loud, because Irma and Mike would beat me up. His clothes were downright disreputable. Not just tacky, but uncouth! I have to be careful in criticizing other folks' clothes, because I get so many compliments on my coat.

"And *she* loves *him?*" My amazement, however, burst out.

"She adores him!" sighed Irma rapturously.

I sighed—*not* rapturously, I assure you! "I will *never* understand human beings! No never! Not *ever!*"

"You don't need to, sweetie," said Irma, with all that cat's wisdom that I'm forced to admit we dogs lack. "They don't understand themselves."

"He looks like a goblin from an unsuccessful fairy tale."

"You might not appeal to him either. And what do you know about fairy tales?"

"The professor teaches them sometimes. He says there's a simple and genuine Philosophy of Life embedded in fairy stories and myths."

"There's also a simple and genuine Philosophy of Life embedded in this furniture store. And it's called Love! So observe—and be quiet!"

The goblin and the goddess made their way to the window. Then Edgar sat behind the chaise longue, out of sight, still holding Brenda's hand, while she exquisitely lounged. He kissed it sometimes. But her other hand was draped demurely towards the window. And it was a beautiful hand! People gawked at that hand!

I began to feel queasy. But Irma got misty-eyed—quite uncatlike, in fact. Mike watched with realistic detachment. He'd seen more of life than any of us, including Edgar and Brenda Blan-*deen*.

I didn't feel altogether overjoyed, and not even a little bit proud of myself, at the thought of eavesdropping. And especially eavesdropping on two young human beings who *loved* one another. But Irma had said that I might learn something, so I kept on shushing my conscience with that.

Brenda said, "I took forty-one words in dictation last night."

Edgar said, "My accounting is the most accurate in the class." From behind the chaise longue, where he hid, he squeezed her hand tighter.

Brenda said, "With our next money, do you think I could buy a typewriter?"

Edgar said, "Sure, hon'. I can get my textbooks secondhand."

"Oh, no! I don't want you using any messy old textbooks!"

And—would you believe it?—they went on like this for three quarters of an hour! Her classes, his classes; her progress, his progress. And I was expecting Philosophy. Deep insights into The Human Condition.

But then—it was strange—I began to see *through*. Through all the nonsense they talked about, through the words they used, and even through their thoughts. I stopped hearing idiotic comments on typing and certified public accounting. I heard only voices: Brenda's and Edgar's. And I must have begun to look funny, too, because all of a sudden I realized that Irma Cat was staring at me.

"You seem very intent," she commented dryly.

"Well, it's so funny."

"What is, my furry philosopher?"

"When the human beings fall in love—" Professor T had never said this, and I dreaded to make a fool of myself.

"*Yes?*" Irma insisted.

"It's just—if two of them are in love, then *everything* gets interesting! They could talk about the furniture. You'd think it was Aristotle and his girl—no, Plato—discussing the World of Sublime Ideas."

Irma said not a word. However, she did allow herself a private and lengthy smile at Mike.

"Yeah, man," the canary said. "But it's da same fah ev'yone! Should be, at leas'. Take me, now. Da foist few mont's, before her mind stahted droppin' stitches, my ol' lady tried to knit. She'd knitted in her past, I guess. An' man!—I woulda tooken it up myself, if da claws was able ta woik dat way."

These reflections—which seem quite important, in retrospect—were abruptly interrupted. A door slammed in the back of the store; heavy footsteps approached. Edgar extracted one last kiss, dropped Brenda's hand, and started to rearrange furniture. Any table or chair would do, as long as he could seem very busy. Brenda shifted position—an arm, a leg—and concentrated on the window, where she hoped the prospective buyers would be. Irma sighed, frustrated, and Mike kicked over a lavender cushion.

"It's Rodney Sturder," said my cat. "What a drag he is! This is something else you can learn: don't ever be a Rodney Sturder."

"Irma! My word! And after all! I'm not a puppy!"

Rodney Sturder tromped up, an overweight mutt—if I say so myself—of a man. He was middle-aged, which is necessary sometimes, and had a pot belly, which isn't necessary at all. And he was bald and had a beard. But the weird thing is, both his being bald—his absence of hair—and his bushy beard—a toomuchness of hair—both seemed like a disguise. There was something hiding inside that head. Under his baldness, behind his beard, there was something I just didn't like—right away!

"Any customers?" he demanded to know.

"Not yet, Mr. Sturder," said Edgar apologetically.

Rodney Sturder cast an eye like a flashlight around his boutique. "Working hard, Edgar, huh? Forgot about all those chairs in the back room, unpacked."

And then he became downright vicious. "You [swearword] dopes! The front door's not unlocked! I give you [swearword] [swearword] dopes a dinner break, and the two of you don't open the door. How in [swearword] can we get customers, if the [*dreadful* swearword] door's not unlocked?"

Even *my* ears, which I clamped tight shut, couldn't block out the horrible language he used.

"I'm honestly sorry, Mr.—" poor Edgar began to apologize.

"It's *my* fault!" said Brenda, leaping in, in defense of her lover.

"You came in together, you went out together. You're always together. And now, kiddies mine, you're *fired* together!"

"Oh, Irma!" I whispered. This kind of human violence upsets me even more—no, very *much* more—than an old-fashioned dogfight. One of which I was in—and lost—in New Haven. But that's another—and very unnerving—story.

"*Shh!*" ordered Irma.

Rodney Sturder removed a cigar—an unlit, very messy and chomped-on cigar—from his mouth. His lips looked messy and chomped-on too. *Yecch!*—how I didn't like that man! "On second thought"—as if he'd had more than one!—"the beautiful Brenda can stay. If that should by any chance be her wish." His smile oiled into a leer.

"I'll go!" the lovely lady pronounced.

"You've got till Friday! That is, if the both of you want a week's pay. Then Brenda goes—or Brenda stays. Maybe stays with a raise. But the football fullback"—a cruel cut at Edgar's skinniness!—"he's out! Now get in the back room, Mr. America, and start unloading those footstools!" Rodney Sturder,

with ugly looks—but of two different kinds—silenced both the
goddess and the good goblin. . . . And then he stalked off.

"Don't worry, hon'!" said Edgar, for Brenda had started to
cry. "We'll make out."

"I won't stay! Without you."

Edgar then did a thing that a sensitive dog could appreciate:
he just let his fingertips graze her hair. (We like that too.)
"We'll decide by Friday." He went to the back of the store, and to
work.

"You wait," Irma ordered Mike and me. She jumped up into
Brenda's lap and snuggled and stretched along one arm.

"Oh *there* you are, catcat," said Brenda, through her tears.

Irma arched her back and walked her fur over Brenda's
cheek. (There are so many ways—and thank Heaven there
are!—that tears can be dried.) Irma said, "Meow!" in a way
that any human being would know meant "Just wait! I'll be
back."

She jumped down to Mike and me again. "You guys get out
of here now. We've got problems. To be fired—you just don't
know. For the humans, it's the worst."

"Can't I help?" I said, and wished, but doubted, in this ugly
web of human intrigue.

"Just go home," said Irma. "I'll walk you out."

We paused at the door to Rodney's office. He was trying to
light his sloppy cigar, which kept spluttering—the nasty wet
thing! He swore at it like an enemy. But it wouldn't be lit. I was
glad.

Then I thought I heard a splash. "What's that?"

"It's just Sarah," said Irma. "You got your bag?"

"Who is Sarah?"

"Some dumb goldfish named Sarah. See her in that medi-
cine jar over there? On Rodney's desk. The former owner of the
store forgot to take her when he sold out. My Brenda feeds her
once in a while. I don't know why. She must be old, as goldfish
go. And that jar is a disgrace."

I knew why. I saw Miss Sarah Gold. She was elegant and
pretty and nice.

Sarah Gold Fish had style. I peeked at her, around the door's corner. And *I* think that Sarah was thinking of *me!* She stopped her swimming, poised like an arrow in my direction—and something happened. We two became friends, just in that one glance. Her elegant tail waved very slowly, in a way that said clearly, "Oh yes! I know you."

And my own stubby tail wagged, "Yes! Me too!"

"Hurry up, please!" said Irma. "My Brenda is simply miserable. I've got to comfort her."

I looked at Irma—so nervous, so eager for Mike and me to leave. And I looked at Sarah Gold—so knowing who I was.

"Come back if you can," Irma Cat called over her shoulder. "Before Friday, though."

"Oh, I'll be back," I said.

ELEVEN

Rabies!

The next week was one of those awful times when human worry or fear or pain spills over and makes us animals wretched too. A death in the family will always do it, and so will the threat of losing a job. I know how I'd feel if Professor T got sacked. (Except he can't: he's got tenure.) Of course neither Brenda nor Edgar owned Irma Cat—nobody would ever own *her* again!—but she had decided that she owned *them*, and the thought of their coming unemployment—no jobs, no money, no studies—my word!—made her absolutely miserable. Because she really loved those two. And a cat's love is very strange. Believe you me, I know! They seem so aloof, but they care—oh, they care!

Mike and I were seeing quite a lot of each other these days— "the attraction of opposites," one might say, or "furs and feathers can also be friends." Mike had time to spare, because his old lady slept most of the day, and the nighttime too, as far as that goes, and I could more or less make my own hours. A little woofing, a little wagging—the professor and Mrs. T don't need much.

So Big Mikey and I hatched this grand idea. We thought that if we hung around the furniture boutique and kept staring up, as fascinated as we could be, at that big glass window, behind which were lounging Irma and Brenda—why, then we might collect a crowd. The curious human beings—for people are always curious—would want to see what we were staring at; the crowd would get bigger; they'd go inside; Rod Sturder would then appreciate what prizes he had in Brenda and Irma; he'd change his mind; et cetera.

The trouble was, tough though Big Mike is, he still is quite little, and very often he almost got stepped on. And me—even with my trusty bag, I still was scared of the dogcatcher. . . . Oh well, as Plato said—or at least he should have—some ideas are sublime, and others are just a bust.

And Friday, like a dentist appointment, came nearer and nearer. Most human beings like Friday. It means, for the next two days, they get to goof off. But none of us five—two humans and three sympathetic animals—enjoyed the approach of the end of that week. It was like the dreary tramp of doom.

On Friday afternoon at the boutique, Mike and I did really give it our best shot. Mike flew up and pecked against the glass, and yours truly barked like the Bone of the World was at hand. A few people stopped, but mostly to laugh at us. Beyond the window the elaborate lounging of Brenda and Irma, so graceful and ingratiating at first, had turned into the postures of pure despair. Which also were very beautiful—but you had to have an eye for it. Tragedy is grand—if one knows how to take it.

Irma knew what we were doing, of course, but I guess Brenda just thought we were nuts. Edgar worked in the back, not wanting to lose his last week's pay. And Rodney Sturder—that idiot!—kept pounding on the glass from inside and shouting "Shoo!"—or vile, unprintable human words to the same insensitive effect. I often asked myself, on that memorable afternoon, if the human beings, really, were worth it! But then I decided: yes, a few are.

The hour for Brenda's and Edgar's dinner break came. All week Big Rod—except he was just big and fat; there are all sorts of ways to be "big," you know—Big Rod had kept on insinuating to Brenda how he would make it well worth her while if she remained and "let the bug-eyed little scarecrow take off." And just because Edgar wore glasses. The wretch! Or "da bum!" as Mike would say.

Mike's own last solution—which he offered very seriously—was to fly all the way to the top of the storeroom, then dive-bomb down on Rodney Sturder—"like a falcon I'll come! An' da bum'll wake up a mont' from now. In Bellevue!" (A hospital—and not the nicest.) But that seemed too violent—even for Mikey Canary, I mean.

So off, hand in hand, went Brenda Blan-*deen* and Edgar Veasy, to enjoy, if they could, their very last hamburger as employed human beings.

Mike and I creepy-crept around the back and into the store. Irma Cat was lying so despondently on the chaise longue—which still hadn't been sold—that I thought the only human beings she might attract were hospital attendants or under-takers.

"All is lost," she moaned, and a paw drooped even more gloomily.

"Ya want me ta boin da place down?" asked Mike. "A joik like dat—wit' his cigars—dey's gotta be matches somewheah!"

"Oh, Mike, you really are too much!" I exclaimed. "Now arson—my word. Although much of this modern furniture is not to my taste."

"Well"—he flicked his tail feathers—"I almost didn't mean it."

"Besides the danger," added Irma. "No—fire is out. Whether or not this stuff is no good, I also hate waste."

I was glad. Just glad for the *things.* The chairs, tables, sofas, the old faithful chaise longue—they gave out a silence and a still sorrow. Unbought furniture, like unlived lives, can be very depressing. You just know that each item feels personally rejected. But also, like lives, they all still have a chance. Destruction is absolutely *out!*

In the stillness, which went on and on—and on!—somebody had to say something. I myself was about to leap into the pit of our silent embarrassment, when back in the storeroom we heard a muffled creaky crack: a door opening.

"Whazzat?" Mike was all alert.

"*Shhh!*" whispered Irma.

For no reason at all, except that I always expect the worst, I began to get panic-stricken.

"That's not Rodney or Brenda, or Edgar!" said Irma. Her triangular ears both peaked to an even sharper point. "Let's just duck—very fast!—behind that modular couch!"

"What is modular?" I thought, if I talked, I could quiet my fear.

"Just hide! Anywhere!" said Irma. And she and Mike vanished behind the modular couch. Which I found out later means, comes in pieces.

And I vanished too, in back of a black canvas chair that looked like a broken butterfly. I say "vanished," but of course I knew all the time where I was. And I knew I was terrified.

There were six of them. Thieves! And believe you me, even if there had been one more, nobody could ever have mistaken those goons for the seven adorable dwarfs. I never saw such a collection of two-legged trash in my life! The ones who weren't big and ugly and dangerous were little and ugly—and dangerous.

From where Mike and Irma had vanished, I heard the two of them whispering. By padding softly and carefully—which is something I'm really very good at, with the nice soft pads I have on my feet—and choosing my time, I was able to join them. They both were peeking around the corner of that modular couch, Irma's head above Mike's.

"Now *dat*," said Mike Canary, in a voice I thought was *much* too loud, "is da saddest sack a criminals I evah saw in my whole feadda'd life."

"*Shhh! Shhh!*" I whispered urgently.

"It's an inside job," muttered Irma. "You see that one with the red bandana? He used to help Edgar unload the stuff. Until Rodney caught him trying to kidnap a card table. He knows the hours—that's why they're all here now, him and his unlovely friends."

"Get a load a dat short little noivous numbah. Da one

wit' da hair at shouldah lengt'. I nevah seen such a ridicalous robbery!"

"How many robberies have you seen?" I couldn't help asking.

"Enough!" Mike's laugh was deep and hearty and rich—like everything else about the dear bird—but just now it made me *terribly* nervous!

"I think—if we creep very close to the wall—and keep quiet!—we can make the back door." My plan, though perilous, seemed the only workable one, to me.

Mike and Irma retracted their heads from their peeking, behind an ugly puce couch, and stared at me.

"You think we just should—leave? Run away?"

"An' dem bums robbin' ev'yt'ing?"

"Well, yes. Of course." I glanced, hardheaded and realistic, from one to the other. "It's the only logical thing to do. *Escape!* And right now!"

Irma fiddled with her whiskers a minute—sort of toyed with them with her right front paw. Mike leaned on a wing and just stared at me.

"Is that what they taught you at Yale?" asked Ms. Cat. "In Professor T's enlightened courses in Greek, Chinese, and Armenian Philosophy?"

"There's no need to be offensive!"

"You just hoist your hind legs and run away? While a robbery's going down? Beautiful!"

"Now listen here, Irma," I announced, more loudly than I'd intended, "I'm as brave as the next dog!"

"Oh, him."

"Yes I am! But this isn't *our* affair! In the first place—let's be rational—this isn't our store."

"I happen to work here—"

"As a friend to a girl who's about to be fired. A lovely girl, I grant you that, but at best—and by her own choice!—a Middle Western secretary!"

"Peck him, Mike! Peck him *hard!*"

"And in the second place, this store is owned by a human

being who even by human standards, debased as they are, is
awful! And in the third place—no, second and a half—quite a
bit of this furniture is modern and ugly and horrible. Who
cares if it gets stolen? Not I! And in the third place—"

"How high do youz t'ink he can count?" said Mike.

"In the *third* place—and this is it—" I brought all my doggy
honesty into my soulful eyes. *"What can we do?* Against six
thieves? What *can* we three do? A cat, who's trying to find
herself. A canary, who has, I admit, the soul of an eagle.
And—and—"

"An' a cockerel spaniel who's got da spots scared off his
behin' right now," said Mike.

"That wasn't necessary!"

"Run along, puppy dog." Was there sadness in Irma's voice?
Disappointment? There are times when sadness hurts more
than a hurt. "Just creep alongside the wall—you'll get home
safe and sound." She clicked her eyes onto Mike's. "You take
the three little ones. I'll zero in on that big zombie with the
rhinestone earring—the klutz!"

"Now just a moment!" I fairly shouted, forgetting my terror.
"I know when I'm being accused of cowardice!"

"Oh, do you?" purred Irma. "I thought we might have to hit
you with something."

"Despite what you may think of me—" A floundering feeling,
like someone drowning, was sloshing all around in my chest; it
even gulped up into my throat. "What *can* we three do? Even
courage oughtn't to be foolish, you know. But I'll try—"

"Da retoin a da cockerel," said Mike.

We were silent, but we were together again.

"We can't attack them," I explained. "Too many, too big." I
think at that moment I did the very hardest thinking I've ever
done in my life. (And, given the results, I shall never think that
hard again!) "If there were just something—some way an
animal like us—could scare the hair off a human being—"

And then Irma—or else it was Bastet, you subtle Cat
Goddess!—came up with a really suprahuman idea. No dog
would have thought of it, that I know!

"There *is* one thing all humans fear."

"What?" "What?" Mike and I spoke both at once.

"Rabies!"

Just the thought froze the marrow inside my bones!

"They're petrified of it!" Irma continued.

"So am *I!*"

"You just have to pretend."

"Me? *I?* I won't! And why I? *Cats* get rabies."

"It's far more alarming in dogs."

"It alarms *this* dog! I can tell you that! And the whole thing's absurd. I *always* have my inoculations. For everything! Vitamins too, if I should looked peakéd. Even if the T's forget— I always find some way to remind them."

"You only have to froth a little. You'll scare the blue jeans off them."

"Don't canaries get rabies?" I hoped aloud.

"None dat I know of poisonally," said Mike.

"No, wait!" Irma's tail was a whirlwind of imagination. "I've just had another great thought!"

"Mange?" I pleaded. "That would be far less drastic."

"Go into the men's room! There's soap in there—"

That really was too much! "In all my life I have never been in a lavatory!"

"There's always a first time. For everything!" the kitcat reminded me. "Now, in the men's room there is a sink. And two faucets. There is also a bar of soap."

"And just how," I asked, "did a female cat acquire this information?"

"I snoop," said Irma, and went right on. "You just push on the faucet with your paddy-cake paws, and then lather your lips—"

"With *soap?* Used by human *hands? Rodney Sturder's hands? Are you mad?"*

"—and then charge out behaving crazy. I mean, not like crazy the way you are, but an outgoing crazy: foam, froth, barking, growls—the whole bit."

"This is simply the most ridiculous—"

"I t'ink it's a swell idea," said Mike. He clapped me on the back with a wing. "Big Jer, dis is one of dose times dat separate da men from da dogs."

"Well, I'm a dog!" I reminded him. "And nobody—except maybe another 'cockerel'—is scared of a cocker spaniel, not even one with rabies! And even then, I'd have to be bigger—"

"Get inta dat john!" Mike's wing compelled me towards a corner of the furniture store, where I saw a ghastly and unclean door with a sign on it that threatened: MEN.

"Oh, I can't!" My head reeled, my voice squealed, and my legs just buckled under me. "No. No! This will all end in tears!"

"What doesn't?" said Mike. "Come out like Godzilla, babe!" He gave me one last, irresistible push. "An' meanwhile, me an' Oima will create some distractions."

The first phase of Mikey's distractions was to seize in his bill one corner of a singularly unattractive cushion, fly it up in the air, and then drop it—*plop!*—on the biggest burglar's head. He of the hideous rhinestone earring!

"Hey, man!" the goon said. "There's somethin' weird goin' down here, man!"

And little did he know!

I shan't even attempt to describe the horrors of that uncleaned, unsanitary, and altogether uncivilized lavatory. For modesty forbids such descriptions. Suffice it to say—a horrid place! With things that aren't at all necessary scrawled over every wall. Why do human beings do this? No dog would.

I knocked down the top of the you-know-what, then jumped up and looked over into the sink. Unwashed for days! Mike's and his ol' lady's kitchen, stuck off in their slum apartment somewhere, was a hospital by comparison. (But a *true* slum is only in the mind.) The soap, a foul-smelling yellow brand, looked more like a cake of dirt. I was used to Ivory. And *I* was supposed to lather up my face with this?

Oh, Irma! The things one does for—

Well, it was do or die. It was foam and froth, or fail those who were depending on me. I pushed on the water and waited while the soap became soft. Then—*Yecch!* The thought of it still makes me gag! I pawed some suds all over my face. The smell was offensive—so of course I sneezed. Which wasn't too lucky, since I swallowed some soap. Then I *really did* froth! And foam! And gag! And choke! And I very much doubt if rabies itself could be worse. I was a sight!

How much of a sight I didn't even know myself, until Mike peck-pecked at the partially open door and flew in. "What's keepin' you, man? I'm runnin' out of upholstery to bomb on dem, an'—*holy Moses!*" His wings collapsed and he dropped straight down on the very luckily lowered cover of the you-know-what.

"Are you—*shlg!*—satisfied?"

"Take a look at yaself in da mirrah, Godzilla."

I leaned up, and the monster I saw in the streaky mirror above the sink made me yelp myself. Not only was I foaming and frothing at the mouth, but the uk was *yellow*, like the soap! And the more I tried to lick it away, the sudsier it got.

And my eyes! My poor eyes. Some soap had gotten into them, and they'd turned a cheery, cherry red . . . no, scarlet . . . no, fire-engine—well, let me just say that no red like my eyes had ever before been seen on this planet!

And my ears! My poor furry ears, so floppy and soft—I've always been so careful about them: mites and ticks, you know—my ears too were sloshing in yellow slush.

And my *nose!* I refuse to go on. The disgust one sometimes feels at oneself is really the worst disgust of all.

"Youz look *bee-oo-de-ful!*" said Mike.

"I think I may throw up," I warned.

"Wait! Wait!" Mike fluttered from his unlovely perch and into the air again. "Do it outside, pal! In front of dem bums. Ya got your rabid roars all ready?"

"*Shlg!—Glk!*"

"Dat'll do, dat'll do. Now bare yer fangs!"

"I don't have—*llk!*—fangs. I have very well maintained teeth and gums."

"Okay, okay! Ya ready now?" He hovered by the door. "On ya mahk—get set—an' go, *man*, go!"

I burst forth: the one and only cocker-spaniel—rabid—dragon ever seen in all New York. And I roared, I can tell you,

but mostly because I had swallowed the soap and thought I might be choking to death.

"Grrr!" Or sounds to that effect.

Even Irma, who'd been howling bansheewise, to distract the thieves, left off her screeching and stared, amazed.

I had meant to dash back and forth, creating an impression of uncontrolled delirium, but by now my eyes were so enflamed the delirium *was* uncontrolled. And it hurt. I started stumbling over things. That hurt too. Heaven knows, there are lots of sharp corners on most modern furniture!

However, I am forced to admit, with all due modesty, my effect on the goons was electrifying.

"Mad dog!" one screamed.

"Mad dog!" "Mad dog!" They all took up the cry.

"Rrrr! Grrr!" I growled. The last time I had growled so successfully, I was being choked by a lout of a cop. This time I was retching on yellow suds.

"Mad dog! Mad dog!"

One especially weird thief-creep, who had glazed eyes—he *could* have been one of the Seven Dwarfs!—took a different view. He kept musing, "Oh man! Oh wow! Like—a mad dog—wow! That's *really* far out! You're a trip, Fido, babe, you're really a trip!"

Behind my lather and my burning eyes, my heart had to smile, a little, at that. A mad dog—me! And I've always been known as the sanest spaniel in all of southern Connecticut.

My delight in this ludicrous situation was somewhat curtailed, however, when I heard the biggest, most vicious of the brigands declare, "We gotta kill him! If anyone of us gets bit, it's curtains!"

Policemen, thieves—there are so many people who want to kill me! You would think I'd offended them, somehow.

The goon picked up a wrought iron chair, a tacky outdoor item, and aimed it at me.

Now, costume parties, even when one is dressed up as Godzilla, are lots of fun. But having your brains bashed out—by an iron chair shaped like a lyre, at that, and wielded by a goon with one rhinestone earring—is altogether a different thing. And not at all desirable!

If I was to depart this life and Rodney Sturder's furniture store so inauspiciously, however, it was going to be over the two dead bodies of my best friends. Irma leaped, and fastened her claws on the leg of the brute, and Mike Canary, whom I'd come to think of as being an angel in disguise, now became a woodpecker! He landed—*thump*—straight on the back of the big villain's dirty neck, and started to drill a hole in it.

At this point in time, and having crept under a green leather couch, I decided that my duty was done. I wanted *out!* And rapidly! But I hadn't counted upon the cruelty and craftiness of thieves and curs and murderers! It never does pay to trust even the most innocent-appearing crook! The thief I'd thought was the most timid and nervous yanked a knife from his belt. But poor, degraded human being—perhaps he was really afraid of rabies. "There he is!" he yelled in terror. "Down there!"

Before I could spit soap at him to show that I wasn't really infected, or maybe just to blind him for a moment or two, this human weasel had actually stabbed me! And right in my—well, where I sit when I've drawn my hind legs under.

"Ouch!" I hollered. In dog, of course. To the thieves it just sounded like a really humongous bark.

Mike plunged at least twenty-six feet and attacked my attacker—who was bulging halfway out from beneath the green couch—in exactly the spot where he had jabbed me. *Justice!* I thought, even then, in my pain. And if my behin' hurts, I cruelly wished my attacker, well I hope yours does too!

And I really was smarting. Where-I-sit-down was sore. I looked around and saw—I was bleeding! And there's only one thing that is worse than the blood of someone else—your own blood. When you see that you're bleeding, there are two things you can do: you can pull yourself together, or faint.

I had made up *my* mind, when so many things happened—so many sounds, so much commotion—that passing out simply skipped my mind.

For Brenda and Edgar came back from their dinner break. Which they'd taken, I found out later, at the local McDonald's.

"What's going on here?" asked Edgar in a voice that rang out with more courage than I knew the boy felt.

"Oh help! Police!" shrieked Brenda. "It's a robbery!

It was now what the less distinguished newspapers would call a fair fight: six idiotic, but nonetheless dangerous criminals against the five of us—two terrified human beings and we three stalwart animals.

We had at it with a will! Edgar, slender though he was, did heroic deeds with a pair of andirons. And Brenda got in a few darn good licks with a big brass candlestick. Mike Canary drilled and bored and pecked. Irma scratched and clawed. And I, yours truly—and modesty will not prevent my telling the truth—why, I was the real hero of the hour. With my foaming face and my guttural roars—I still was choking on soap, you know—I had the brigands petrified.

I must add, however, that the act that really ended the fray was Edgar's pressing a yellow button, near the front of the store, that was labeled: ALARM! Which sound set off a clanging I thought would crack all the glass in the store.

The thieves fled.

Our Brenda and Edgar hugged one another.

"Let's split," said Irma. "This mess will be hard enough to explain."

"No, wait!" I commanded. (Yes—commanded!) "I have an idea." I guess the suds had gone to my head.

Before Mike or Irma could say "Tweet! Tweet!" or "Meow!" I had dashed up to Edgar and rubbed my bleeding you-know-where on his pants. He and Brenda were dumbstruck; they didn't move. When he was sufficiently ruddy and bloody, and thoroughly a mess, I ran back to my allies.

"Now what was that all about?" said Irma.

"You have *your* plans, and I have mine! Now shall we—or shall we not—*run!*"

We ran, the three of us: two on foot, and Mikey Canary running, featherfoot, through the air. Escape! Escape! After Victory!

The last thing I heard, in the storeroom in the back, was that same splash I had heard before. I looked up. And there she was again: Miss Sarah Gold Fish. Her eyes, though gray, seemed to me to sparkle as brightly as her golden scales. I had to pause.

"Will you *come?*" said Irma. "It's just that dopey goldfish."

"She's beautiful!" I said.

Then, midstream in this current of altogether human confusion, the cops began to arrive. And we animals—like the crooks—fled.

The difference was, we animals—bless us—were *free!*

TWELVE

Miss Sarah Gold

In the swift narrative of my life in New York—which *I*, at least, find very exciting—there are some characters of greater importance (yours truly) (but Irma too) and others of less significance. Like Big John, the cop, who is huge, to be sure, but apart from saving my life that time, not really a major figure at all. Despite how Irma fawns on him! And makes me mad when she does it too! But I come now, with some embarrassment, to a genuinely inconsequential little soul. A sort of a—kind of a—well, I mean an embarrassing little friend of mine. Except that I still find her beautiful—and love her, disinterestedly, without pause for myself.

Oh, whiskers! This is going to be difficult. And really embarrassing for me too. But embarrassment, my gentle and attentive friends, is something I know *all* about! Heaven knows—I've been embarrassed so much of the time, it's the climate of my life, by now.

This awkward pause in my New York adventures began the day after I went rabid. And there was no need of my bag *that* day! You should have seen all the panic-stricken New Yorkers jumping aside as Irma and Mike and I dashed home! But luckily no dogcatchers saw me. With my slathering lips I'd have been whisked off to that ghastly place on Twelfth Avenue for sure!

We reached the Thompsons' cellar safely. Luckily again, they were both away, at a tea for a visiting Russian poet. For an hour I gargled, while Mike and Irma jabbered on about all the thrilling events of the day.

But at last Irma said, "Will you stop that, please! You sound like a third-rate dramatic soprano warming up for the Metropolitan Opera."

"If *you'd* just had rabies—"

"You didn't have rabies. You had a mouthful of soap."

"Which is worse! And I also got stabbed"—I would not be denied my dramatic moment!—"and my blood flowed!"

"So wash your behind. And stop gargling."

So much for my heroism! But anyway, the soap was gone, the blood washed away—and I wanted to get in on the jabbering too. It's really delightful to talk about danger, as long as it isn't there anymore.

It was ever so late before Mike flew home. "Oh, boys!" he exclaimed. "I fahgot da ol' lady! So long, youz guys—"

It was even later when Irma and I went to bed. Our jabber had turned into reminiscing—that is, to tranquil recollections —and then to just the sudden jumps and the fun of remembering. We petered off into yawns and laughs. And then we nodded on into sleep. We were happy together, even in sleep, because both of us trusted that what we'd done was right—in the proper animal way—as well as exciting.

The next day I was one furry bundle (with brown and white patches: my coloring) of sheer curiosity! What had happened? To Brenda? To Edgar? To Rodney? To Rodney's big fat ugly cigar? To those kooky criminals? And, most especially, to my reputation: the rabid dog who had foiled the dastardly robbery? And even more most especially—had my plan worked? The blood and stuff. Only *I* knew what I had meant to do.

I barely could eat my Milk Bone that morning.

At ten-thirty Irma was back. She had slithered out through the crack of dawn to gather what information she could. And shortly after, Mike Canary flew in. He had finished his chores with his beloved old lady early, and he too had flown out to reconnoiter.

"You are a hero!" said Irma. "Almost."

"Yeah. One dat dey want to gas," said Mike.

"Oh dear. And I thought this one time it might not really end in tears."

"Tears, fears—who cares?" said Irma Cat. "It's Life, puppy-dog. The papers all say a mad dog interrupted a robbery. And the cops caught the crooks, who were falling all over each other escaping down Perry Street. Big John was there too! A hero, as ever. He collared that creep with the earring."

"I thought *I* was the hero?"

But Irma ignored me and went right on. "Some guy even snapped a picture of us. It's in the cheap papers"—she sniffed a bit— "but not the *Times*."

"But bein' rabid, aftah dey pins da medal on youz, youz goes to—"

"Please stop. What a world," I philosophized. "It all goes wrong. Nothing works as you want."

"But it didn't go wrong!" said Irma. "Your mouth is now free of soap—at last!—and they don't know who or where you are. You're as safe as an owl at the North Pole!"

"That's a curious comparison. I mean, why should an owl—a barn owl, hoot owl, or any owl—be safe there? But yes, perhaps a snow owl—"

"Will youz listen? Ya mutt!" Mike gave me a warning peck on the head. "Youz is safe! An' ya plan—which now we *unnastan'*! —it woiked! Dat blood on da goofball—"

"'Edgar,' he's called. And I like him."

"Nat'rally!—youz two bein' goofballs. Dat blood on da goof-ball Edgah has *woiked!* Nex' to youz he's da hero of da day!"

"It appears," said Irma, "to the newspapers and also the perceptive police, that Edgar—little good goblin Edgar— arrived at the right time, when the rabid dog had the thieves at bay, and completed the victory. He even was—"

"*Wounded!*" I triumphed proudly, and rather loudly. "The blood proved that."

"Youz is some cockerel." Mike shook his head, in rather insulting disbelief. "A dopey dog, from Connecticut. An' a hero."

And Irma, ironic as always, was forced to agree. "Youz is some cockerel." She flickered my whiskers with her tail. "But Edgar—the honest goblin he is—he tried to deny it."

"Oh no!" I groaned. "And all my work. And my foresight—"

"Ya behin', too," said Mike.

"—my well-laid plan." I fixed Mike with a spaniel stare. "And yes, my little feathered friend—my *injury* too! All gone for naught."

"Don't worry," said Cat. "The cops and reporters wouldn't believe him. When this city needs a real-life hero, they manufacture one. There is even a—"

"Reward?" I breathed. Just barely had I hoped for that! Not that I expected to see a dime myself.

"And a huge one!" said Irma. "Big John proposed the idea to Rodney Sturder. And Miss Brenda Blan-*deen* and Mr. Edgar Veasy—who now are publicly engaged!—have announced that they will use the money, this fabulous, unearned reward—"

"*I* earned it! Although Big John, of course, had the bright idea!"

"—they will use the well-earned sum to complete their education!"

"In typin' an' arit'matic!"

"And *then* they will move to their very own linoleum Heaven in the Middle West."

"Teentsy-weentsy as it is!" said Mike. He hit one wing against the wall. "Da joiks! Dey could have been on television! Commoishals! *Fame!*"

"Control yourself, littlebill," said Irma. "It's what they want."

Now right about now I really was feeling quite like Godzilla, or Lassie, or the Alpo Dog. Or King Kong! I was Dog of Dogs! And the admiration of cats as well—so I'd hoped. Just *all* my schemes and dreams had come true! But then—fool me—I had to ask, "And how is Miss Sarah Gold? That fish—"

"Oh, and that's another thing," said Irma. "Rodney's selling the furniture store. This boutique freak from Madison Avenue showed up and offered to buy the whole mess. 'The publicity,' I heard him crooning, as he fingered an ugly ring all by himself, gazing out the window."

"But Sarah—"

"The last I heard," Ms. Cat said casually, avoiding my everpresent eyes, "Rodney Sturder had told somebody to flush her down the john."

"*What!*" I leaped towards the window—and fortunately it was now open—and dashed, bagless (but at this critical juncture, who cared?) towards Greenwich Avenue. Fast!

I'd like to philosophize—but I won't. I was in a hurry.

To the rescue ran I! Her pale gray eyes seemed to plead with me: help! I raced across streets—against stoplights too. As long as I was a hero, I thought, Why not risk everything? But how many heroes, I wonder, know just what they're getting into? Not many, I'll bet. Well, at least I knew where I was going: to *Rodney Sturder's Furniture Boutique.*

The place was chaos! The police were still there, messing things up in a vain attempt to discover what else had been stolen. Big John was *not* there, however. At least I was spared that prickly annoyance. And of course nothing *had* been stolen; we animals had seen to that. The new owner, whose name was Wyatt Neil, was also there, inspecting the store he had purchased. I would guess it was more than he'd bargained for: his face was pale, and his mustache drooped. But maybe it was meant to droop—*I* don't know! All I could think of was Sarah Gold Fish.

Most luckily it never occurred to anyone that this nervous cocker spaniel (me) who kept tripping over everything was the rabid dog of yesterday. Much animal welfare depends, you know, on the lack of attention of human beings. But trip I did—and, at last, tripped into the room where Sarah resided. I had feared to hear the sound of flushing, but—thank Heaven, and the god of all fishes!—there she still was!

Now, communicating with fish is difficult at best. Unless you're another fish, or maybe a waterbug, but to talk to them is out of the question—even for an animal. (Porpoises may prove an exception.) Yet Sarah and I had what the French poodles

call rapport. That means, we understand one another without feeling a need to speak.

The rapport that Sarah and I had, told me, through her eyes,
that she had felt simply scared to death. She sensed all that
was happening, and—fins and scales!—was she ever glad to
see me! To be just simply flushed away would be quite bad
enough, but ending by going down the drain in *that* lavatory
would be adding insult to injury.

However, now that I saw that Sarah Gold Fish still was safe,
temporarily, one little detail did occur to me: how was I going to
make her safe forever—or at least for the life span of a normal,
healthy, and alluring goldfish? In fact, I suddenly realized, how
could I guarantee her safety for the next ten minutes? The
bumbling in the showroom came nearer. I had visions of
hands—the tough, though well-meaning hands of cops, and
Rodney Sturder's vulgar hands (he had a diamond ring: fake!
fake!) and the fidgety hands of the new owner, Wyatt Neil. I
had waking nightmares of these hands lifting Sarah's bowl,
then carrying it—oh no!

I jumped up on the table beside her. "Miss Sarah," I said,
"you don't know me—and I don't know you—but I'm here to
help you, if I can."

Her tail wagged back and forth furiously. Which I took to be
fish talk for "Yes!"

"Now I don't know if this will work," I explained, "but it's all I
can think of. I know that I'm only a cocker spaniel—and also
I've just come to New York—"

Her tail flashed up and down: fish for "*Please* shut up!"—
as best I could interpret it. One final flick: "Just *do* something,
for scales' sake!"

"All right," I agreed. "Now, what I'm going to do is this— No,
first look in my mouth." I opened my mouth and displayed
what any dentist would love to see. "My teeth aren't too
sharp—I mean, they're sharp enough for a steak bone now
and then—" Flash! flicker! in her bowl. "But I'm going to take
you in my mouth, with a mouthful of water, and take you
home."

The sidewise tail-waggle showed me, I hoped, that she'd understood.

"You'll have to not move, or else I'll gag. I gag quite easily." Wag! wag!—up and down. "Oh, all right—here we go. But be still—if you can."

In a life that's been weird and wonderful since coming to New York, this must have been my grandest and my maddest hour!

I plunged my head into that goldfish bowl—felt Sarah swim inside, then rest quietly—water flowed in with and after her—I shut my mouth—and it was done!

Except for my nose. I began to leak. But, as with our ears, we cocker spaniels have secret ways of closing our nose. I did so—after taking a monstrous breath. It would have to last me three and a half blocks. No—four! I forgot Tenth Street.

Can anyone ever describe my dash home? Yes, I can! And I will. With a fish in my mouth. And on only one breath. The stops. And starts. The red and green lights, you know: I obeyed them this time, because to open my mouth for any explanation would have meant quick death for Sarah Gold Fish. And me too, probably. The traffic. The casual steppers-on-paws. The mounting frenzy! Oh, *would* my lungs explode?

Well, I was the mostest *me* in those few minutes: heroic and terrified—and expecting it all would end in tears.

But it didn't. Not yet.

I reached our backyard, dove through the window, and vomited Sarah into the sink. Please excuse that word—no other will do. Then I collapsed, a panting wreck. But I still retained enough canine sense to put my paw over the drain. I'd saved my dear from one drain, by whiskers!—and I wasn't about to let the gold darling disappear down another!

Mike Canary and Irma Cat were still there. The whole operation—don't they say that in adventure films?—had taken no more than ten minutes, and I assume that the two of them had been wondering what in Greenwich Village had happened! At any rate, they were both astounded when I disgorged Miss Sarah Gold.

"*Mmmm!*"—from Cat.

"I t'ought I'd seen ev'yt'ing!"—from Canary.

"Miss Irma Cat, Mr. Mike Canary—" Gaspingly, I remembered my manners. "I'd like you to meet—Miss Sarah Gold."

Another interruption now. Because it gets downright ugly from here. Unanimal. Almost human, in fact.

"Would one of you please turn on the faucet?"

Oh, whiskers!—and scales and fins too!—was I ever cool and collected! My friends were still absolutely astonished, from seeing me spit out a goldfish, so I thought I'd make the most of it by being as normal and nonchalant as a frantic cocker spaniel can be.

"Irma—please?"

With a rather peculiar Bastet expression, as if she was trying to figure out something, Ms. Cat pawed on the hot water.

"Really, Irma! Cool. Not too warm! I'll test it, please." Which I did, with my free paw. And Irma's eyes got greener and greener. Boy, oh boy!

"So what now?" said the kittycat. "You going to keep your paw on that drain until some fisherman comes in and catches Miss Sarah Gold?"

I ignored her. "Mike, would you flit through the cellar—"

"I don't flit, bud! Not even fah youz. I *fly!*"

"Would you wing your way through the premises, and see if that eagle eye of yours can spot a suitable container. That shelf above the clothes dryer—perhaps there—"

"Yeah. Full of doity bottles."

"If Ms. Cat and you could manage to lift one into this sink—and rinse it, please." I knew, of course, that Mikey Canary, big as he is, couldn't lift a great big glass jar—so Irma would have to, and that made me laugh inside. Because I, nat'rally, with my paw on the drain, couldn't help at all.

She rassled a jar from the shelf, and couldn't quite break it, since it fell on her back. And then the two of them eased it and lowered it into the sink. "*Yecch!*" said Missy Kitty. "It's filthy! It stinks."

"Mmm," I purred, "it'll take quite a lot of washing."

She glared; Mike chortled; and both of them washed.

"Just a minute, my dear," I said encouragingly to Miss Sarah. "We'll have it all ready and clean for you. When those two get finished with their scrubbing. And don't you be frightened—I have a firm paw."

"Oh, firm!" echoed Irma, while she scrubbed. "Like a marshmallow firm!"

When I had been satisfied that the jar was quite clean—a big job too: it took time, which I liked—we tipped it on its side. Miss Sarah lunged against the current, as I very carefully lifted my paw—and in the slithering cutey swam. Then carefully we righted that jar. I urged my cat to be most cautious.

"There, there," I crooned to Sarah Gold. "You're safe. And don't you worry about a thing. We'll get some sand, or some pebbles—or something—whatever you'd like in your new home. And Mikey Canary will being birdseed. If he can feed his lovely old lady, he surely can help to feed you. And Irma—" I gave her a cat look—as much of a one as this dog could muster. "Irma can ask her friend Big John what he thinks a beautiful goldfish could use. That is, if he can tear his attention from any other animal." A sharp glance here—and you know where! "You rest now, Miss Sarah. Such an aristocratic name: Sarah Gold."

"Her name is Fish!" said Irma Cat. "Miss Sarah Gold *Fish!*"

"But 'Fish' is such a tacky name," I explained, "for someone so elegant. I'm going to call her Sarah Gold. And just you remember, Ms. Irma *Cat!*—Miss Sarah Gold belongs to me! So don't you go reverting to type! If you don't attack your friendly neighborhood canary, then you can leave my goldfish alone as well! Got that?"

"Mmmm," purred Mike. Everybody was getting catlike today. "Dis is gonna be interestin'!" He folded his wings and looked—interested.

"I'm going to have to do some research," I murmured privately, to myself—but loud enough for Irma to hear. "Perhaps you can help me, Mike?"

"Anyt'ing. Any little ol' t'ing at all." And if birds could grin— well, who's to say they can't?

"You might fly back to that pet shop some time, where you met your own ol' lady, and see what a goldfish eats."

"They eat slimy green things that grow under water," said Irma with distaste, if not malice.

"They do *not!*" I shouted. "They eat lovely dry fish food that comes in a cannister!"

"So why did you ask? Mr. Cannister."

"I—I—well, I wondered if the goldfish in New York were the same as the ones in Connecticut. The professor and Mrs. T had a little fellow a few years ago."

"What happened to it?" the cat asked cynically.

"Unfortunately—*he* died. Of fish flu."

"There's a lot of that going around, I hear." Irma licked her whiskers. "Right here in New York."

"There had better *not,*" I diagnosed, "be any fish flu in this cellar!"

"Um—guys!" Mike interrupted. "Are we leavin' Miss Sarah in her jar in da sink? Or are we movin' her someplace else?"

"If Irma Fat Cat has *her* pet—"

"*Who* are you calling fat? Spaniel-belly!"

"We are *not* fat!—as a breed."

"Well, as a furry person—you *are!*"

"Um—guys—"

"And *what* pet am I supposed to have?"

"To pursue the question, Kittygut: it's just that all those hamburgers and other goodies that that muscle-bound cop is feeding you—"

"Oh! Big John—"

"—have begun to show! And your stomach's dragging!"

"Like [swearword] it is!"

"To resume the discussion: if Irma Fatgut has her pet, why can't I have mine?"

"Boys, oh boys!" sighed Mike. "Dis is gonna be bettah dan I t'ought."

"So it *is* Big John!" Irma's whiskers were bristling. "You're jealous."

"I am not!" said yours truly, in rather too loud a voice. My

composure was vanishing rapidly. "But *I* want *my* pet too!" I
aloofed her—and woofed her—as best I could. "Besides, don't
all the alley cats in New York have big dumb cops for pets?"
Woof, *woof!*

"You cur!"

"Don't say that, Irma." I advanced upon her threateningly.
And whether by instinct or intuition, my lips began to pull
back from my teeth. "That word—*cur*—no self-respecting dog
can stand that."

Mike jumped between us. "I would like to repeat: d'youz
want Miss Sarah Gold in da sink?"

Cat and I backed off. I walked my hind legs under me and
tactfully sat down. "I can't decide. At this critical juncture,
perhaps you have an idea, Mike—"

"And that's another thing!" burst out Irma, who really had
been stung by ever-so-sharp innuendoes. And I was glad—
glad!—GLAD!—do you hear? "Why do you always talk so
phoney? 'This critical juncture' and stuff like that?"

"Ever since we've met"—I let her have it—"that's been the
burr you've got in your fur!"

"I have no burrs—"

"You're *jealous!* Because I'm well-educated!"

"You're a verbal show-off, if that's what you mean."

Mike Canary hopped over and leaned one wing against the
jar. "Miss Sarah—I guess youz remain in da sink." She swam
towards him, and rested her head against the glass, where his
wing rested too.

"She does *not* remain in the sink!" said I. "If I had the help of
some other four-legged creature—who wasn't too clumsy—I
would like to move her into the light. To that corner of the
shelf, over there." I briefly glanced at the only other four-legged
creature who happened to be in the cellar just then.

"Oh, swell!" said the other four-legged creature. "Let's move
her into the light! By all means!"

"One moment—" I stretched up on my hind legs and found
the somewhat rusty top to the jar. "I'll just wash this off—"
Which I did. "And screw it on—" Which I also did, very neatly

too, by using my teeth. "And there we are. To prevent accidents."

"Now, youz two four-legged critters, be careful!" Mike had a premonition, alas. And even more alas—it came true!

As Irma and I were lifting the jar, she on one side and I on the other, I thought I felt a little push. At any rate, I fell—*smack!*—flat on my back. However—and thank Heaven, and all my whiskers too!—I knew enough to hug the jar on top of me. On my tummy, that is. Which indeed and alas was soft enough to keep it from breaking.

It didn't break. Miss Sarah was safe. I heaved a breath of sheer relief—and then righted the jar gently. It stood on the floor. Miss Sarah, I think, had had palpitations. She was wiggling distractedly. But she too knew she would be all right. She'd been hugged to me, after all!

I faced the four-legged—*thing!*—and barked. "You did that on purpose—you feline fiend."

"I did nothing. You slipped."

"It's true, what they say! All cats are self-serving—"

"And dogs are dumb—"

"—and altogether selfish. Besides which—you're a gossip and a common scold!"

"You're sentimental! Lapping hands—a sentimental mutt!"

"Alley cat!"

"Mutt! Cur!"

"Okay, youz guys." Mike held up two of our paws, as if testing. "It's gotta be! Now come out sluggin'! But nuttin' doity—or undah da tummy."

"And what do you think *you're* talking about?" screeched Irma Cat. "You little yellow nitwit, you!" She was, I am happy to say in retrospect, absolutely beside herself. Just out of her mind! In a frenzy of fury . . . I loved it even then. She cared enough. I had made her mad.

"Easy, gal," Mike said to her. "I don't want to beat up on no pussycat. An' expecially a frien'. But I have in da past. An' I can again. So—*boing!*" He struck an imaginary bell with his wing.

Now here begins the true and unending embarrassment. I mean, the real thing! What you hide from the mirror. Irma Cat, who had left the Nussters because she was bored by mediocrity—and Jerry Cocker Spaniel, who'd attended lectures on Greek philosophy—we had a furious, very real, very hurtful and common and ordinary cat-and-dog fight! . . . The shame of it! Oh!

I bit her tail. She tried to bite mine—and missed. For which I was very glad. It's rather short, you understand: a characteristic of my breed—but it *feels!* But then she got a good clawhold on my rump. That *hurt!* I reared, and roared around. Her throat was exposed. I lunged towards it. Her other claw was above my eyes.

"Okay. Dat's it."

We heard a voice. And felt two wings. They separated us, very gently.

"Youz guys are too much!" He shook his head, canarywise. "You *mean* dis fight!"

The shame of it . . .

One four-legged creature, who looked as ashamed as *I* was, slunk through the window. And vanished, with her tail held low.

The other four-legged creature, whose tail could not be held low—not enough of it—just crept into his corner and closed his eyes.

And a bird flew home—to a sadness he hadn't expected so soon.

THIRTEEN

Mike's New
Young Ol' Lady

To howl—or not to howl: that was the question. It frequently is, when you lead a dog's life.

The thing about shame is, it stays! Like the mange. Or anything else horrible. Until it gets treated.

For one solid week—and that week felt as solid as a block of concrete, with me trapped inside—I felt ashamed. I went for my daily walk with my bag—sometimes the professor took me to class—but alone, with whomever, or just in the cellar, I felt as if Shame had a leash on me. . . . Who would have believed that the first time anyone called me "bad dog!" it was I myself who called myself that?

Not a word did I hear from Irma. Not a yowl, not a single meow. Mike Canary dropped in, but infrequently. His ol' lady was sick, he said—the poor bird. He looked worried and harried, and his chirp didn't sound too hearty to me. But nothing sounded hearty to me—least of all my own bark when I heard suspicious noises at night. I still had my duties to attend to, you see. But even work, which usually takes one's mind off bad times—at least keeps one from brooding—even my job didn't work for me. And neither did taking care of Miss

Sarah: feeding her various kinds of scraps—some of which I had snitched—and adding more water to what had evaporated. I think she knew something was wrong, but I couldn't *communicate*. And didn't try.

Oh, but I attempted to avoid the humiliation that haunted me like a constant ghost—you bet I did! I tried other feelings where I could hide, and the shame not find me. For instance, I could feel self-righteous. Ha! ha! ha! And, she had it coming! Who, me?—be *wrong?* . . . Or self-defense. I wasn't so bad. Bow-wow. Pet me, please. . . . Or, worst of all, who *cares? Grr!* Who gives a [swearword]! I could try to be cruel and cold and indifferent. The way the humans often are.

Well, for better or worse, nothing worked. By the end of the week I just lay, hour by hour, in a great big emotional puddle: pure misery! The question wasn't even whether to howl, anymore. It was, to whimper or not to whimper? To cry—or just die?

Was ever a dog as depressed as I? But then the answer occurred to me: yes! This is one of the uses of suffering: you realize that other dogs have to do it too. And a few human beings, I suppose. It's a hard way to learn. However—it's the only way.

By Saturday I had made up my mind to creep down to the Charles Street Police Station, and wait for Big John, and then follow him home—where I knew in my bones Missy Kitty was staying—and hurl myself at her furry feet and plead for forgiveness.

That, fortunately, was not necessary. Such drastic action still rubs my fur the wrong way. For around noon, on that Saturday, in she slunk.

"What are *you* doing here?" I demanded stiffly. "I assume you've come back to hurl yourself at my furry feet and plead for forgiveness." It really is wonderful—I guess—how rapidly Pride returns in this life.

"Where's Mike?" She ignored my question, with all its implications, completely.

"How should I know? Downtown, I suppose."

"He said he'd be here."

"And where have you been, might I ask? At Big John's all week?"

She seemed distracted, preoccupied—as if, in some funny sort of a way, I, Jerry Dog, with all my problems, was not there at all. "I stayed with him for three or four days—"

"May I ask why you left?"

"Just too much country and western music. And those three phoney Angels."

"Oh! Does New York's finest, shiny Big Blue like country and western?" I was going to pooh-pooh Big John's taste in music, but something in Irma's attitude—a dire, impersonal seriousness—froze the irony in my jaws.

"On Thursday I moved in on Mike."

"That's about the last time I saw him. . . . Irma?"

"He said he'd be here—"

"Yeah. I am." Without either one of us noticing him, he had hopped through the window and onto the sill.

"Did they get her?" asked Irma.

"Yeah," said Mike.

"Did *who* get *whom*? And will both of you please stop talking above my head?"

Irma's glance, unaccompanied by a spoken word, said: Do shut up—you're going to feel like a fool as it is.

My eyes must have shown my bafflement, as I tried to question Mike silently.

"My ol' lady died."

We all looked towards the River—the great River—and said nothing.

I felt like a fur coat that's starting to shrink. Do you know how fur shrinks? The cheapest kind? It gets tighter and smaller. And smellier too. An old fur coat does that, in the rain. And I did it too. I just could have died! And wished I had. "Oh, Mike!" I blurted. "I *am* so sorry!"

But then, even worse, I got curious. (The ignominy of one's self!) I wanted to know: how? where? when? and why?

Mike understood. And don't any one of you ever tell *me* that the instinct of a canary bird is not as high as an eagle's flight! He talked. Told me the whole story. I think it helped him to speak it out. (One day—in Professor T's best lecture—he said that anything awful could be endured—that is, you could get through the worst of it—if you could speak it out. Make a story of it—so it had a beginning, a middle, and an end.) Dog that I am, I do know this: to *tell* something is everything!

"Youz know dat she's been sick." He was talking to me, since Irma knew all this already. Except the last, gruesome part. "It wasn't dat her body was sick—but her mind got sloppy an' all mixed up. Even more dan usual. Da past an' da present—wow! What a confustication! What trouble—"

I glanced at Irma. We both were thinking—a confustication, a trouble, a worry—for *all* of us.

"She got on dis kick of rememberin'. One paht of her ol' brain was goin' fast—but anuddah paht was comin' back even fastah. Wow! Did youz know she was married?"

"No!" "No!"—meowed, woofed we together, passionately.

"To a—get dis!—a conductah on da subway! Da one who guides da train. An' her husban' was a conductah from feaddah's knows when! From da foist time dey had subways in New York! Imagine dat time! Da excitement!" Mike's eyes went into the past—and came back. "His name was Franky. I assume dat meant Frank, but she loved him, so Franky. An' dis is what kills me—she rose ev'ywheah just to be wid him. She was rockin' in dat rockin' chair, an' recitin' da stops: Times Square, Penn Station, Foiteent' Street—he must a been on de express—an' she would ride wid him, ev'ywheah! She would ride on his train, so that just them two could be togethah. An' maybe hol' han's between da stops. From one t'ing she said, I t'ink one night dey got as fah as Coney Islan'! An' dat was— gosh on my feaddahs!—back in da toities. Or even da twenties!"

"Before we were born," I heard myself murmur. The time before one was even alive . . . it's so hard to imagine.

"So finally," Mike continued, "an' dis is wheah it gets very not nice—her Franky had an accident."

There was a pause; Mike couldn't speak. He was that upset— for himself, his ol' woman, for Franky too, although none of us had known Franky at all. But during this lull, which swelled our hearts with sadness and love, we became aware of a wiggling. Missy Kitty and I had been so engrossed in Mikey's sad tale, we'd forgotten completely about Miss Sarah.

Fish talk, as I've said, is curious. But fish listening is even curiouser. They hear more than they say—I just know that in my bones. And right at this point—this critical juncture—I realized, with a mammal's shock—my fur stood on end!—that Miss Sarah had heard, or understood, every single word. And a fish's eyes, like canaries' eyes too, can't cry. But oh! can they ever look tragic! She was wiggling in sympathy, pressed next to the glass of her bowl, and her gray eyes sadly reflected Mike's story.

The canary was glad for this interruption. A recess from grief is always welcome. "Hi, Sarah!" He hopped to her jar and patted it with one wing. "Hi, doll! Youz been okay?"

Miss Sarah's wiggling involved her whole slim, elegant self.

"She's even better than your tail! Look, Irma—those curves! —full of cryptic information."

"I'm looking—you canine clown."

"I admit I'm a clown! But how expressive she is! What sympathy! What a fish! What understanding! What—"

"What did happen to Franky, Mike?"

"He got squashed. He was down on da tracks, repairin' a cable—and anuddah train came—" You may think a canary's eyes don't change—that pure black—but they do. They get blacker and sadder.

"Oh—" I closed my eyes.

And "Oh—" Irma Cat did too.

But—nothing: no sound that we heard—Miss Sarah sank to the floor of her jar. And there she lay, deathly still.

"An' my ol' lady was *dere!*" said Mike. "By da way, did I tell you dat her name was May? I foun' dat out because she would quote her Franky—'My dahlin' May!' or 'My dearest May!' She remembahed deir letters. Yeah—" He sighed. "Aftah all dis time—I foun' out dat her name was May."

"Your old lady *saw?*" said Irma.

Mike said, "She was on da train. It was one of deir holdin' han's times. On da way to da Battery. I won't talk about dat no more." He cleared his choked canary throat. "So aftah Franky's

death May lived wid a creepy brothah of hers. A pawnbroker on
Eight' Avanoo. But dey didn't have nuttin' to say to each othah.
Den Newark—New Joisey. A cousin of hers, who was a nerd.
An' *he* didn't have much to say to her, eithah. So den—" A note
of pride lifted Mikey's voice. That is, instead of being a
baritone, he sounded like a dramatic tenor. "So den she
became a bag lady! An' one of da foist in New York. Maybe—
wow—da *very* foist! A pioneer!"

"My word—"

"My whiskers—"

The cat and I were both trying to measure time. "How long
ago—"

"Oh, *very* long!" the canary said impressively. Then he
thought again—and he wasn't so happy. "An' so dat's what she
did, for all dose yeahs—just roam da streets—a scavenger."

"Till she found you!" I burst out uncontrollably. "And you
made her a home! And took care of her! And I love you, Mike—"
I was crying now.

"Easy, kid." Irma rested a paw on my paw.

"But how *horrible* life can be!"

"They found each other at last," said Irma. "Just think of it
philosophically."

I stared at her. "To [swearword] with all philosophy!"

Irma patted my paw, and smiled. "A cockerel spaniel to end
all spaniels!" But in her eyes there was still one matter to be
cleared up. "Did—anyone—come though? Mike? Today?"

"Oh, yeah." The canary finished his story. "When I saw by no
breathin'—an' also by da peace on her face—dat she was
gone—dat's when I tol' you to come up here wit' Jer. I wanted ta
make da final arrangements myself. So's I went out an' foun'
da nearest cop cah."

"I could have gotten Big John—"

"No. It was fah me ta do. I just pecked on da top of da cah—an'
dey followed me, t'inkin', I guess, dat rabies had spread to
canaries too—an' dey foun' her, an' took her—"

"Miss Sarah has fainted!" I interrupted. At least she was
lying down, tummy up, in her jar. And at this point in Mike's

sad narrative—*any* excuse for an interruption would be welcome!

"Hey, Sarah! Hey, hon'!" Mike pounded on her jar wth one wing. And scratched it with a claw—awful sound! "She lived to be a ripe ol' age—an' she died lookin' ovah da Hudson Rivah. Dat really ain't all dat bad. An' da sun was comin' up too, dis mornin'."

Miss Sarah Gold revived. She swam languidly back and forth, as if adjusting to all the unhappiness in the world. Then abruptly—perhaps struck by an intuition—she darted to the glass, to Mike's eyes.

"Hey great! She's poikin' up," said Mike, peering in. "Don't you be miserable now, Miss Sarah! One grief at a time is enough. I know I can't cry—no tears ducts in boids—youz fish are da same—but youz an' me, Sarah—we *feels!* An' by da way, Jer, what's dat crud on da floor of her jah?"

"It's some dog food that she didn't eat."

"Dog food!"

"Mike, *I* don't know where to get seeds or crumbs or ground-up autumn leaves! Or whatever else a goldfish eats."

"So youz bin t'rowin' your own slops in dere?"

"Not slops, I assure you! I pick out the very choicest morsels before I even begin to eat. And also"—this I had to whisper—"I've been pilfering from the mister and missis!"

"As a pilferer youz is a bust!" Mike shook his head. I suspect his own bird question was: to peck or not to peck—my head! He decided not to, fortunately, and said instead, "Youz is da dumbest mutt in New York!"

"Hear! Hear!" said Irma.

"Keep quiet," said I. "Big Mikey can call me that—not you!"

"Put ya foot on da drain, Fido!" said Mike. Which I did. "Now, Oima, very carefully—"

"I get the idea—"

They tipped the jar, then emptied it, and Mike Canary—such strength in those wings!—turned on the faucet. In a minute Miss Sarah was swimming luxuriously in a sink full of water. "*Clean* water!" said Mike. "No dumb dog food in it! Youz stay here—just eggzackly like dat, wid ya foot on da' drain—an' I'll be back."

Without so much as a chirped "Bye now!" he flew through the window.

This was rather a cringe-making time for me. (And I hope for Irma too!) We discussed the weather—rather warm for October; our health—I had found a tick, but called it to Mrs. T's attention. I was just about to ask my ex-friend—or *was* she? I wondered—if she thought my whiskers were turning gray—prematurely, of course—when Mike came back.

In his bill was a little box of fish food. "A sample." Mike set it down. "An' Mr. Gosslah will nevah miss it. He has da pet shop on Hudson Street." Mike perched on the rim of the sink. "How ya doin', sweet Sarah? Dat's a very nice boidbat', dat sink—ain't it?"

Miss Sarah wiggled affirmatively.

"My paw's getting waterlogged," I said.

"So's ya head! Dog food—for a gol'fish!" But this time Mike laughed. And I always love to hear Mike laugh: just like a big ol' human man who is slapping himself on the knee. "Dat looks really nice." Mike wanted to share his pleasure with us. "Jus' look at her swimmin' down dere! Boys—what a day! He fanned his face. "I could do wid a bat' myself."

At that casual wish, which Miss Sarah had overheard—or at least understood—she did a truly remarkable thing. She leaped from the sink and landed beside him, on dry porcelain.

"Miss Sarah!" Mike lifted her gently in his bill and dropped her down in the cool water again. "Youz mustn't do dat. Why dat's—dat's how a fish commits suicide, jumpin' out in dry air."

Then she did it again!

"She's saying something." Cat studied Fish. "She wants something. And I have it! She wants you to take a bath with her!" Without looking at me—no, she wouldn't do that—Irma added, "And it's happened before, in that sink, I believe. Two people having a bath together."

"Is dat it, Sarah?" Mike flexed his wings. "Can I join youz?"

She jumped a Yes.

"Here I come!"

Now, any other canary I know or have heard of, or even dreamed about, would have slipped, perhaps with a little splashing, into a birdbath. But not Mike. He folded his wings behind his back, shouted "Geronimo!"—and then leaped, straight up, and dove, headfirst, into the sink.

There was almost too much—and just barely enough—of joy and laughter and everything good to be kept to one's self. I looked at Irma. She met my eyes, and we mingled our hilarity. For there Mike was, in the brimming sink, being washed—tactfully—by Miss Sarah Gold. Under wings, between claws, et cetera.

That is, *at first* it was tactful. But then there began some tickling. I had never realized, until now, that fish were so good at wiggle-tickling. Miss Sarah was having fits of mirth. She just was in tizzies of squiggles! And Mike was roaring with laughter and orders: "Hey! Quit dat, youz! Now stop!" But of course he didn't mean a word.

You see, Mike Canary was loving it. Miss Sarah Gold was loving it. And Irma and I, who were together, at least and at last in this one thing, were loving it most of all.

It was Bliss! It was furry and feathered Heaven—with fish scales too! In a middle-class cellar. On Charles Street. And on the day the old lady had died. But maybe the Good Dead leave Heaven behind them, as well as going there themselves. And Bliss in a sink doing duty as a birdbath—that really is remarkable! . . . Oh, well, New York is a city just *made* of possibilities.

And things got even more possible! Mike flew up out of the flood and landed on the bridge of my nose. "Youz too! Get in dat boidbat'!"

"Now, Mike!" I was lying down flat on the counter next to and overlooking the sink, where I could reach down one paw on the drain. "I'm fine eggzackly where I am!"

"Youz is gonna get bettah! I hear dogs' noses is sensitive—" He started to squeeze.

"Ow! *Ow!* OW! Oh, all right—" Down I floundered with my usual grace, head first, and came up spluttering.

From his perch on the faucet Mike called up, "I hear dat cats' ears is pinchable too!"

"Mmm. Why fight fate?" murmured Irma Cat. And splashed in herself.

The Goodness and bathwater overflowed.

"I have to say something now," I said. "And Miss Sarah, you have to hear this too."

The wet frolicking stopped. They could tell from my tone I was serious.

"I love you, Miss Sarah—I honestly do." She swam onto my paw, and lay there, at rest. "But I have to admit, when I rescued you—" I could never have said this, except that in so much splashing love, the truth was the only thing possible. "When I rescued you, apart from thinking that you were charming—I wanted to make Irma jealous too." I turned to the cat. There was water dripping from both our whiskers. "And Irma—I guess if you want to stay with Big John—why, that's your right."

She studied me with Bastet eyes, cat goddess eyes that go right through you. "But honey—he's human. He's only a human being."

"Of course," I went on, after clearing my throat, "and that choice will have to be up to you. But if you should want to come back here, and visit sometimes—"

"He's *human,* sweetie! Of course I'll come back! And besides"—with her tail—O lovely tail!—she flicked water up into my nose—"if I heard one more country and western number I might turn into a banjo myself!"

"Well dat—at last—is dat!" said Mike.

"Not quite," I said.

"Ya brains *is* gettin' watahlogged!"

"Today Mike Canary suffered a loss." I was speaking very formally. I always know when I have the floor—even if it's a foot under water. "And this I must ask you, Sarah Gold: although I saved you, would you like to live with Mikey Canary? I mean—like to be his *new,* young ol' lady?"

Sarah flipped off my paw. We could tell she was thinking.

Mike flew to the bridge of my nose again. No squeezing this

time. "Jerry baby," he chirped, in his heartfelt baritone, "Big Jer—would youz do dat? Fah me?"

"I would. It's up to Miss Sarah."

She leaped up in the air—such aim she had!—and kissed me, coming down. We all knew that meant *yes!*

And we all felt so rich, we animals. Who have nothing, really, except ourselves. And a few good human friends.

"As long as we're in here, we may as well wash Miss Sarah's jar. And add a few spices." Even Bliss must be interrupted, in order for it to last.

So the next half hour we washed the jar. Finally, with all kinds of care, we packed it—and Sarah—into a sturdy satchel. My bag wouldn't do for something so heavy, and Mike, with that eagle eye of his, had gone rummaging through the cellar. He found the satchel, which also had to be washed, in a very dusty cupboard. It had printed on it: New York YMCA—1958. A very good year, that must have been. We all were so happy.

Then, getting it out was a bit of a problem. I could hardly leap over all the trash cans that lay in the alley, or bull my way around them either, with a satchel containing a water-filled jar containing one goldfish.

But we all demanded to have good luck that day! We refused to believe in obstacles. And guided by Mike—and Irma too—cat's sense, bird's eyes—we made our way to Perry Street. And I walked very formally—to be careful, of course, but also I felt processional.

Did you know three people can be a parade?. . .

Well, we were, as we marched down Washington Street, to Mike's ugly, beautiful tenement. Each bleary window in every abandoned warehouse we passed seemed like a perfect magic mirror, reflecting the late October sun, as bright as our own happiness.

Did I say "three?" . . . But there was Miss Sarah concealed inside . . .

So if three human beings—or animals—can be a parade, why, four are an absolute celebration!

FOURTEEN

A Witch's Cat at Last

My Irmy had come home! And I thought, in my own dumb-dog way, that my problems were over. Little did I know—or suspect! They only were starting. For this latest Cat Goddess—true daughter of Bastet of old—this witch's [swearword] cat!—she *still* wasn't satisfied.

I had assumed, what with parceling out her time between Big John and me—which I generously allowed—and what with visits to Mike and Miss Sarah—well, any normal feline person would surely have been happy. Not she! In one week's time she came down with the fidgets, and by two weeks—you'd have thought she had fleas!

"It's not enough!" she meowed, and clawed a dishrag that hung above the delightful sink.

"What isn't?"

"Life!"

"You want to take another bath?"

"No, I *don't* want to take another bath!"

It all was even more pitiable because lovely Indian summer was here. The snoozing, in sunlight, was wonderful. The autumn yawns were a perfect joy. We dogs lick our chops in

165

times like these—not to clean any crumbs of dog biscuit away, but just for the pure, sheer joy of it. Oh, if only Irma had had some chops of her own to lick! And those nervous little paws of hers, which she kept wetting and sliding down over her ears and face—if only they'd had an occupation! Very graceful, I must admit—but her face and her ears were *already* clean! If Irma had just had some chops to lick, or an ear to scratch—I mean, not because it itched, but only because it's so relaxing—her career might not have occurred at all. . . .

But it did!

And it started one innocent Sunday morning.

Herself dashed in and yowled, "Guess what! I've got a job!"

"Oh, not another!" groaned himself.

"I'm an actress!"

"A *what?*"

"Last night I was strolling down Macdougal Street—"

"That's a part of the Village I don't like at all!" Already my hackles—*all* of them—were rising suspiciously. "The tourists go there. And freaky people."

"Well freaky or not, there's a little off-off-*off*-Broadway theater located on Macdougal Street." I understood what she meant, I think. Although you may not. The important theaters in New York are all supposed to be on Broadway. Except that they're not. They're on side streets. And the little theaters that aren't on Broadway are *off* Broadway—or *off* off Broadway. Or something like that.

"My, my," I mused. "That sounds about as *off* anything as a little theater can ever get."

"Well, who cares? They're doing a season of Shakespeare."

Now I happen to know who Shakespeare is—although he is not a philosopher. But granted that limitation, he's a very, *very* important person. A playwright. And the biggest, noisiest playwright of all, in fact. The professor sometimes talked about him when he tried to relate Philosophy to Art. But I won't try to do that now. As a matter of fact, I never will. So although I know the name—Shakespeare—I hadn't heard, read, or seen any of his plays. By the bye, Shakespeare's tolerant friends—both living and dead—all call him *The Bard.* They know he would like it.

"Of course"—Irma narrowed her eyes—"I have a sneaky suspicion—"

"When *didn't* you?"

"—that beyond Shakespeare—and don't be so testy!—the actors who formed this company are more interested in being *seen.*"

"Seen?"

"*Seen!* To be seen, for an actor—man, woman, or cat—to be seen is everything! Like by people from Hollywood, for instance. And these actors, as yet, have not been seen. They all think they're undiscovered movie stars. Although lots of them are still waiters and gas station attendants too.

"Oh." Truth either strikes like a lightning flash, or it slowly crushes you like a steamroller. "So I gather a bunch of out-of-work actors are going to mount great-great-*great* classics in an off-off-off-*off* Broadway theater. In order to be *seen.* By a bunch of dumb clucks from the movies."

"And television!"

"Nat'rally."

I'd always held "the theater"—with all its vaunted poetry—in secret suspicion. Mere entertainment. And now my suspicion seemed confirmed.

"And what, may I ask, is to be your role in this band of strolling, or bogged-down, players?"

She was so excited, my irony escaped her. "Our first play's going to be *Macbeth.*"

I hate to display my ignorance. But, although I'd heard the name, I didn't know much about *Macbeth.* "I assume *Macbeth* is a suitable vehicle for these out-of-work celebrities."

"It's a Halloween play," explained Irma. "There're witches and ghosts—"

"And *pumpkins?*"

"No pumpkins." Her whiskers wiggled. "But maybe. If I can have my way—and it *is* October. Anyway, they chose it—Rita and Vic."

"Who?"

"Vic Rex and Rita Bovina. They're the couple who started the company. His real name is Morris Stroke, and hers is Sally Gundy. They're living together." Irma's eyes looked amused—and way far off. "Which in their case, I think, just means they're sharing the same full-length mirror. He's very big, Vic is—but unlike Big John, who just *is* big—Vic's physique seems to shout to the world, " 'Hey, world! Get a load of me!' " And Rita—her best friend lives in that mirror."

"Enough of judgment!" I said. "Who are *you* to—"

"I'm Irma, sweetie!" she cut me off. "And I do judge! It's a characteristic of cats. However—and be that as it may—and who cares?—Vic and Rita decided on *Macbeth*. These three witches—"

"*What* three witches?"

"Anybody's three witches! Don't be so literal! These witches, in the play, suggest to Macbeth, who's a general or a duke or a—"

"Gas station attendant!"

"—that he kill off everyone, and become the king. Of Scotland, I mean. That's where the action takes place."

"Well, that seems reasonable." My irony again. To no avail.

"*But:*"—I could see the plot thicken in Irma's eyes—"he doesn't have the guts."

"Thank heaven!"

"*But*: his wife does!"

"Is this where you come in?"

"For the second time. I'm also playing—among other roles—the three witches' cat."

"Can't they each afford one cat of their own?"

"Please! With me they need only one. My name is Graymalkin."

"Oh, really, Irma! Does anyone take this seriously? A cat has a name like Puss, or Peachy, if the color is right."

"It's traditional!" She put me down. "Graymalkin is a witch's cat!"

"Oh, well then." I walked my hind legs under, and sat on my haunches. And also my doubts.

"So as well as being the witches' cat, I'm also playing Ms. Macbeth's dear pet. Who urges her to urge her husband, by purring and various other things—"

"To kill everybody. Did you have to audition for this part?"

"No, just to kill one old king—Duncan, by name—and then Ms. Macbeth would be a *queen!*"

"It gets clearer and clearer." In fact, I was more and more confused. I decided to give up on the plot.

"But then she collapses. Nat'rally. She's a human being, after all—"

"In my opinion—"

"—and she gets this guilt feeling. Goes nuts, in fact. She all of a sudden gets queasy and queer, and gets a dose of guilty conscience. And I get to play the conscience too!"

"You? Guilty—"

"I can act anything! We have this terrific scene together! Then Ms. Macbeth dies. The mister too. Everybody dies."

"Do you?"

"Do I ever! And I've got something special planned. But think of it, Jerry! *Three* parts I play!"

I thought. And my thoughts were long and deep. And suggested severe misgivings. "May I ask how you met these strange folk?"

"I was moseying down Macdougal Street—"

"I wish you'd avoid that part of the Village!"

"—and remember that photograph in the papers? From when we caught the burglars?"

"Yes—"

"Well, Choo-Choo Melons recognized me."

"Beg pardon?"

"*Choo-Choo Melons!*"

"That too, I assume, is a pseudonym. At least I hope—"

"Her real name is Chita Melonotti. But Chita became Choo-Choo, for simplicity and the fun of it. And Melonotti—"

"For reasons that escape me completely!"

"—became Melons. It's easier. So it's Choo-Choo Melons. She recognized me. And also, being a witch—"

"A witch? What else—on Macdougal Street!"

"She plays a witch. And a lady-in-waiting."

"Waiting on *what?*"

"On Ms. Macbeth! Now *will* you stop being so literal! Having recognized me, she thought of all the newspapers"—and here Irma switched her tail—"and how much I might add." Her tail dwindled into a compliment. Too modest, her tail was, to say just *who* might be getting this compliment!

"Well, now!" I scratched my right ear with my right hind leg. Which is what a dog does under difficult circumstances. "So you're going to be an actress—"

"Oh, baby!—am I ever!"

I scratched even harder. Because, as I've said: even the worst can get *even worse.* . . . Which was exactly what happened with Irma's and my experience with the Rex and Bovina Theater Group!

For the next few days, while Vic and Rita and Choo-Choo *et al* were rehearsing, I didn't see much of Irma. Some nights she'd come back, late, exhausted, but a lot of nights she stayed in the theater—sleeping, as I found out later, in a witch's cauldron, to soak up atmosphere. And luckily, atmosphere was all there was in it.

Mike and Irma and I had decided by mutual agreement—and Irma's orders—that Canary and I would stay away until opening night. "To receive the experience fresh," she said. "With the bloom on it." Her talk became very flowery just about now. The dangerous influence of Shakespeare, I guessed. One night she stretched her neck dramatically and sort of crooned, "Oh, would that I had a voice of fire."

"But Irma," I reminded her, "if you had a voice of fire, you'd only burn your throat."

"You creep!" she screamed. "You have no soul!"

And I would have been glad to discuss the Problem of *The Soul*—but once you get into poetry, there's just no talking with anyone. Not reasonably, I mean. That's why I've always been somewhat suspicious of the stuff.

So Mike and I waited for opening night. He waited with excitement and glee, and I waited with worry. Among other worries, I didn't want my dearest friend to make an idiot of herself. And finally the night came! And as it turned out, both Mikey and I were right.

Mike knew the way to the Globetown Playhouse, which the Rex and Bovina Theater Group had rented for as long as they could afford. That night, as we wended our way along, all I could see was long hair and blue jeans and crazy dresses, and I actually felt overdressed myself in my well-groomed, brown and white cocker spaniel coat. Dogs too can get mugged, you know! And held for ransom. And all kinds of horrible things can happen to them!

I tried not to be too severe in my judgment, but the Globetown *Playhouse!* . . . Words fail me! And they rarely do. My first thought was, if there should be a fire—and Heaven forbid!—but I had to know where the exits were. At the first smell of smoke, I planned to bark—and hoped someone would say, "*Save the pets!*" The whole place was just about as big as a little living room of a very modest home. And backstage —that's where the actors get crazy, preparing to go "on stage" —well, all *I* can say is, the lavatory of Rodney Sturder's Furniture Boutique seemed like a vast natural park in comparison.

Irma met us at the door. "Come round here," she said, and led us through a musty alley. "This takes us backstage. I want you to watch the show from there."

"Ya noivous?" said Mike.

"I'm not nervous," said Irma. "I'm scared straight out of my fur!"

"Aw—don't be, kid."

"My costume isn't right."

"*What* costume?" I asked. "You're a cat. You have fur. And it's very becoming." Her burnt gold, amber coloring has always been one of Ms. Kitty's very greatest charms—at least as far as I'm concerned.

"But in the first scene I'm a witch's cat!" I had never seen her so flurried and flustered.

"Well, can't a witch—a respectable witch—have a fashionable—"

"Oh, shut up! . . . I'm sorry, sweetie—" Her glances were

dashing everywhere. "You don't understand. These are bad, nasty, evil and ugly old witches!"

"Then why would you want to associate with them?"

"Mike! Peck him!" said Irma. "Or rather—don't bother. It wouldn't do any good. There's no poetry in his soul. But *there!*" Her eyes lit on a filthy trash barrel.

"Is there poetry in *there?*" I asked.

It was one of those big, ugly oil drums, like the one on the way to Mike's. "There's got to be some ashes in there!" said Irma.

Before Mike or I could shout "Help!" or "Stop!" or "Call the Police!"—she had jumped in that barrel. Gray clouds, fumes—pollution!—arose. Then out jumped Irma. She was blackened, grayed and begrimed: in short, a mess—her lovely hair soiled.

"Do I look like a witch's cat now, Mike?"

"Yeah." Mike appraised her skeptically. "A witch widout a dime ta her name."

"Oh, Irma!" I wailed. "Your beautiful fur!"

"I'll do anything for my art!" To prove her point—to me, or herself, or Shakespeare, perhaps—she dove in again. And came out even worse. "Just wait until Choo-Choo sees Gray-malkin now! You guys get backstage. The show's going to start!"

"Oh, Irma, this will all end—"

"Mike—if flop-ears talks while the play is in progress, just knock him unconscious."

"Okay, babe!" Mike gave her a wing-whack on the back. "Knock 'em dead, doll!"

Irma dashed through the stage door. And, as it turned out afterwards, she dashed into immortality, fame—whatever it is that the human beings think most of.

"Come on, floppy-face, funny-ears!" Mike clapped a wing around my back. He sensed how unnerved I was by all this. "Let's go an' see da show!"

FIFTEEN

At Home with the Macbeths

Well, *Macbeth* really *is* a Halloween play. And a few pumpkins would have helped this production.

There wasn't a curtain in this theater. If there had been one, there'd have been no room for the actors or the audience. The lights went down, on a bunch of humans—mostly friends and relatives of the cast—huddled on hard-backed chairs, and in the darkness a heart-shaking screech was heard: our very own Irma, playing Graymalkin! And I still don't see why even a witch's cat couldn't have a nice name like Nancy or Anne!

Mike and I were cramped in a corner of what was supposed to be backstage—part indoors, part alley, part up on a ladder for very dramatic entrances. The so-called actors never bothered about us at all. Either Irma got them all to believe this was going to be an *Animal Macbeth,* or else they assumed that like various other types we had just wandered in from Macdougal Street.

That screech, though—my word! It made my hackles rise. Do humans have hackles, I wonder? No matter.

"Dat's her!" Mike nudged me with a wing.

The lights went up, and there the three witches were.

175

Strange costumes! Kind of shredded seaweed, you might describe them. But nobody saw the witches at all! For there was Irma, screeching and tearing around the stage like a Labrador retriever was after her. The witches tried to say something—about Macbeth being on the way—but after Irma, they'd all have been an anticlimax. And anyway it was only "exposition." That's stuff that the audience has to know, but boring—so it was short.

Then the lights went out—Scene One was over. And I was thinking I might enjoy the play, if all the scenes would be this quick.

Irma dashed to us. "Well? What did you think?"

"Terrifik!" said Mike.

"Ear-splitting," said I. "About that shriek—did they *make* you do that? Like squeeze your tail?"

"Of course not. As every rehearsal I started the show with my scariest scream. Every time. And since they couldn't get me to stop—"

"I see."

"In the next scene, Duncan, the king of Scotland, comes in. He's old and wise and kind and good—so Mr. and Mrs. Macbeth decide to do him in. So Macbeth can be king."

"That is truly appalling!"

"It's *drama*, sweetie!"

"Is he played by an old and kind and wise—"

"No. Felipe—Felipe Luciano—is only sixteen. Choo-Choo discovered him on the Avenue of the Americas."

"And does he speak English?"

"With an accent."

"Scottish?"

"We're hoping so."

I will not describe the entire play of *Macbeth*. Too gruesome. I found it offensive. And I don't like horror movies on the TV, either!

There were the witches' scenes, and the scenes in which Ms. Macbeth—who was played by our very own Rita Bovina— sashayed out and murmured, "We gotta do something!" Or

Shakespearean words to that effect. And that usually meant, "Hey, Macbeth, let's snuff somebody! More for us!" But since it was a tragedy, nobody seemed to mind too much. I tell you—if this had been real life, I'd have called the police—Big John or that likable sergeant—right away!

Irma's next big scene was when Ms. Macbeth got to read a letter. Her husband had written—oh, what does it matter? They had to get rid of Felipe Luciano—King Duncan, that is— so he wrote, saying, "Are you game?" And she answered back: "You *bet!*" Just old-fashioned *thugs,* in funny costumes, is what the Macbeths both were! I'd never have let them in the house!

And here Irma played the evil ambition of Ms. Macbeth. She'd jumped in the trash can again, and came out with a slinky white streak in her hair. She was really supposed to be Ms. Macbeth's pet cat, who should have been licking her whiskers clean, but as the idea of being a queen took hold of Ms. M, Irma's character changed dramatically.

There seems to be something about a throne that really brings out the worst in a person. As Ms. Macbeth got the idea "queen" in her head, our Irma stalked and prowled around her, purring like a bad-tempered dragon. She was speaking cat, but the audience certainly got the idea. "Right on!" someone shouted. I envied them their enthusiasm, because, to me, the plot seemed quite trashy—unlike The Bard's words, which were wonderful!

So King Duncan came for the weekend and Act One ended.

Next, Macbeth was supposed to snuff King Duncan, offstage. But there was an awful crash, which meant that either Mac had tripped or else decided to do in the king by tipping a bureau over on him. He came out— "all shook up," as Mike said, but Rita and Irma screeched at him to finish the job. I was hoping he would have second thoughts. But he didn't. Poor Duncan got mutalized.

And that was Act Two, more or less. And not a single life too long!

Irma's next great scene—but not her greatest—had to do

with the witches' cauldron—pot, kettle, whatever you want to call the thing. They were cooking up something that I don't recommend to anyone!

These witches, who were just three women with nothing better to do, were having a little get-together. "Round about the cauldron go!" they sang discordantly. And round about this steaming pot went Choo-Choo Melons, Elizabeth Natches, and Tanya Tinski, the latter being two young girls also "discovered" on the Avenue of the Americas to fill out the company. That avenue must be awash with undiscovered movie stars!

The point of this scene was that Mr. Macbeth kept coming back to ask the girls what to do. The advice they did give him! It made my fur crawl.

"Dis is wheah Oima gets ta play da Cat Incahnation of Evil," whispered Mike.

"Oh, dear."

The girls were throwing things into the pot. "Eye of newt—toe of frog—mummy dust—"

"Is *that* what witches eat?" I exclaimed.

"No! Dey can it, an' sell it to supamahkets! Now *will* youz shut up?"

The Cat Incarnation of Evil was going around the cauldron too. And every time Mr. Macbeth asked a question, before any witch could answer him, Cat would jump up and down, and screech and moan. And she seemed to convince him that the best thing he could do was to do his worst! The Incarnation of Evil was also loud. But I suppose most Evil is.

I was very relieved when *that* scene was over. "Is that all?" I whispered.

"No," said Mike. "Oima walks in her sleep. Wid Mrs. Macbet'."

"Well, I'll bark and wake them up!"

"Deys *supposed* to be walkin' in deir sleep—ya furry-face, dumb-head mutt!"

The sleepwalking scene was the one in which Ms. Macbeth got queasy. She was having bad dreams—very richly deserved! —so she took to roaming around the palace backyard, remembering her crimes and saying, "Golly—I wish we hadn't done

that!" I'd known she would come to a very bad end, and I had
no sympathy for her at all. She wasn't one bit like the missis I
love.

But Irma had to have sympathy. She was playing Ms.
Macbeth's guilty conscience. So whenever the latter groaned
or sighed, our kitty would give a demonstration of just how
painful a thing it is to be wicked, and not nice. She cried, she
sobbed, she banged her head on a pillar nearby—which was
made of cardboard. I rather liked this part of the play: I thought
it might do the audience *good!* Poor Rita, as Ms. Macbeth, was
wandering around with a lighted candle, and trying her best
not to set the Globetown Playhouse on fire, but she didn't have
a chance against Irma. She'd start a speech, and then Irma
would drown it with a wail, screech, or shriek. I believe, in the
theater, this is called "upstaging" another performer. But the
audience loved it like crazy. The lights went down, and
everyone clapped as if they'd been at a good Dog Show.

Irma raced backstage. "*Well?* How did you like it?"

"Youz was terrifik! *Terrifik!*"

"Yes. Very impressive. Quite frightening, in fact. Do we'z get
to go home now?"

"And miss my *death scene?*"

"Oh." I walked my hind legs under me. "I hadn't realized—"

"Just you wait!"

The Bard had Ms. Macbeth do her dying offstage. I still don't
know what got her at last. That guilty conscience, I trust and
hope! But that wouldn't do for the kitty at all.

Mr. Macbeth and a bunch of his hoodlum friends were
sitting around, complaining and moping, and waiting for
some war or other to start. When suddenly, from offstage, there
came a scream! And I tell you, it must have broken glass all over
New York.

"What the devil's that racket?" said Mr. Macbeth. And I
suspect he had meant to say, in a very poetic voice, "Oh now do
pray tell me—*et cetera.*" But it didn't come out that way.

Some bum friend of his said, "It is the cry of—women?" But
he didn't sound one bit convinced.

And well might he *not* be convinced! Because it was not the

cry of women! It was the cry of Irma, that's who! The Bard
might have wanted Ms. Macbeth to die in her bedroom or in
her bathroom—wherever illegal queens go to die—but not
Irma. She died onstage.

And she didn't walk on. She jumped! From that ladder in the
wings. And did three somersaults before hitting the floor. I
don't think this part had been rehearsed, because Mr. Macbeth and his dubious buddies just stared at her, aghast. She
thrashed, she frothed, she screamed bloody murder—talk
about rabies!—then finally, and at last, and none too soon—
she died, with one last howl. And lay on her back, with her stiff
legs sticking straight up in the air.

The audience simply went out of their minds! I was sure that
that was the end of the play. And it certainly should have been,
because all the battles and other stuff that came after were
really a letdown.

Everybody in the cast would certainly have been mad at
Irma, except that even the dumbest actor—and there are a lot
of that type—knew that it was she that made the show. The
applause—the cheering—the standing ovation—it all was for
Ms. Kittycat! The new Star of Macdougal Street.

"*Now* can we leave?" I pitifully asked.

We were sitting backstage, and everyone was cooling down,
as everybody has to do, when the show is over.

"Just let me savor these moments!" said Irma.

Vic and Rita were cooling down too. Being true Greenwich
Villagers, they didn't think it strange at all that their feline star
had a dog and a husky canary for friends. They were mopping
each other's brows, and doing some smooching, being so close,
as they congratulated one another.

"We've gotta use that cat in *Antony and Cleopatra*," said
Vic. "She'll make the play!"

"Yeah," agreed Rita. "She'll be my—Cleopatra's—cat!"

Then Fate—which is very unlikable sometimes—struck
hard at the Globetown Playhouse—and me!

"We ought to have a dog," said Vic. "For Antony."

As soon as I heard that simple word—*dog*—right then I
should have fled.

Too late . . .

Irma Cat was staring at me. "Mm-*hmm!*" she purred.

Then everyone was staring at me.

"Irmy, dear . . ." I walked my hind legs out from under. "I think I'll be going home now—"

She approached me with staring eyes. They were glazed and glassy with dreadful intention. "Mm-*mm!*"—meaning, "Oh, no, you're not!"

And there began the terror of my celebrity—much worse than the dogcatcher!

SIXTEEN

Between Engagements

"Between engagements" is what actors tell each other they are when they're out of work. As applied to yours truly, the phrase meant that I was tied to a pipe at the Globetown Playhouse, to keep me from making a getaway, and forced to be in the really confusing play called *Antony and Cleopatra.* Or perhaps I should say, confusing classic. The plot's even more tangled than *Macbeth.*

That very first night, when *Macbeth* was over and they got the idea—right then I should have lit out for the hills. (If they do have any hills in New York.) Or else I should have taken Amtrak back to Connecticut. But no. Instead of fleeing for my life, I just went home with Irma Cat—the latest off-off-*off* Broadway star.

All night, while I tried to get to sleep, she kept telling me about this "absolutely marvey play!"

"Are there witches and ghosts in it?"

"No. It's about kings and queens and generals and things. Cleopatra is the queen of Egypt—"

"Oh, *Egypt* again! Do you play a cat goddess?"

"No, sweetie," she purred, and I felt the syrup of her sweet urging pour all over me. She really wanted me in that show. "I play Cleopatra's pet cat, as Rita suggested."

"What is the name of Cleopatra's pet cat?"

"*Mavis!* Or Laverne! How the [swearword] do I know?" The syrup turned somewhat sour here. "What difference does it make?"

"I just wanted to know."

"And *you* will be Antony's dog. Named Fido, or Fritz, or whatever you want."

"Who's Antony?"

"A Roman general. It all takes place in the olden times. You know, togas and pillars and all that jazz. And Antony, this general from Rome, has a mad, crazy, passionate love affair with Cleopatra, the queen of Egypt!"

"They sound pretty old."

"They are. Middle-aged."

"So in other words it's about these trashy middle-aged characters who try to behave like teenagers."

"You *might*—if you were an idiot—describe one of The Bard's very greatest achievements in those words, yes."

"Well, I think it's nasty! Dogs should be dogs, and cats should be cats, and middle-age human beings—"

"Should what? Ride around in their wheelchairs and beat each other over the head with their canes? You're such a prude!"

"I am not! Professor Thompson, in a very affectionate moment, once chucked me under the chin and said, "My word, Jerry, you *are* a salty dog! That was when the poodle—Gladys—lived next door in New Haven. Such charm, she had!"

"Spare me your sordid history!"

"I just want you to know—I've *lived!*"

"So live it up now! And be a star! You can—in this play."

"Oh, Irmy—" But the truth will out.

"I've *asked* you not to call me that!"

"—I'm scared! I have stage fright. The missis once tried to enter me in a dog show. A little neighborhood dog show it was. But I got so scared—I whimpered and cried, and covered my eyes with my paws—that she couldn't bear leading me up on the stage. And in front of all *these* people? In *New York?* In a *play?* It isn't simply the vulgarity of the subject—"

"Oh boy!" Her whiskers seemed to curl a bit.

"—but I'm *scared!* Just as much as of the Dogcatcher."

She laid a paw across my paw—a gesture I cannot resist—and her eyes flashed like the tenderest lightning. "I'll be there!" A glance from those eyes—ah, how they do light up a cellar! Even the clothes dryer shone in their glow.

"I'll think about it."

"You'll do it—you mutt! Or I'll pull out every brown and white hair on your rump!"

On the other paw—she can be quite aggressive too. . . .

So I gave in. I *always* give in! But just in case, they chained me to *that* pipe. At night I was allowed to go home—but only in Irma's custody. She spoke many soothing further words—and sometimes threatened to wring my neck—but she got me back to rehearsals each day.

And the Thompsons—you have no idea how little even the very best owners know of their pets!—they didn't suspect a thing.

I got scareder and scareder. When I wasn't chained up, I was forced to strut, fret, and generally make myself absurd, for my own little hour upon the stage. And was I ever mystified!

I'm not even going to *try* to justify the plot of this play. Just let me sum it all up by saying that Antony and Cleopatra wanted to be King and Queen of the World. But some guy named Octavius, who was even sneakier than those two, he wanted the whole works for himself. And he got it too, in the end—the bum! But not before the action had moved from Egypt to Rome, then back to Egypt, then off to some ocean somewhere, where there was a great big naval battle! That meant that everyone backstage screamed and poured buckets of water all over each other.

Irma Cat kept telling me that the action didn't really matter: it was just the love of these two people that did. But I kept thinking: Love may be fun, but you ought to know what's *happening!* And understand it, if at all possible. However, I know I'm old-fashioned.

My one real joy and consolation during these trying days— apart from Mike, who flew in now and then—was Herman Garter Snake.

Since you'd never grasp the plot of this play anyway, I can tell you what happens in the end. Antony, who's just lost a battle— he loses a lot—tries to do himself in by falling on his sword. And he misses. He botches that, but dies later on anyway. In tragedy they all die—later on. And Cleopatra—would you believe it?—she kills herself by hiring a snake to bite her! An asp, that Egyptian snake is called. A singularly unlovely creature! *Ugh!* I say! What a way to go! And since this production was featuring aimals, Ol' Vic and Rita decided to get a real snake. That also gave the company an excellent excuse to go on a picnic one Sunday.

So Monday morning, when Irma and I showed up, there was poor Herman in a wicker basket. And I cannot imagine another garter snake—or any other living soul—looking quite so miserable.

He stared at us from behind wicker bars. "What are *you* doing here? Did they kidnap you too?"

My soul cried "Yes!" but my voice only said, "I'm playing Antony's cocker spaniel. My name is Jerry. And this is Irma— Cleopatra's cat."

"I'm playing the asp," said Herman sadly. "I'm supposed to be an Egyptian snake that bites some queen or other. As if I'd ever do such a thing!"

"I think that that is *divine!*" said Irma. "I call that really creative stagecraft!"

"I call it cruelty to animals," said Herman.

Irma went off to rehearse some scene where she and Rita try to thicken the plot. As if it wasn't concrete already! And Herman and I got to know each other.

"It was the October sun," he sighed. "That's what did me in. It's so beautiful in New Jersey."

"Connecticut too," I remembered wistfully.

"And I came out on my favorite rock—to sop up the last of it—and these goony New Yorkers appeared, with their picnic. If only I'd moved! But my second-favorite rock has a ridge, and it isn't nearly as comfortable. Besides, they were half a pasture away. But I fell asleep. And the next thing I knew that big tall skinny one there—"

"Felipe Luciano. He was the king of Scotland."

"He was?" said Herman. "That's strange. Because now what he wants to be is a professional basketball player."

"I think, perhaps, he's better suited for basketball than the crown of Scotland. And I'm *sure* that he would enjoy it more."

"I learned all about his basketball playing in the pickle jar."

"What?"

"He grabbed me while I was still asleep. '*Olé!*' he shouted. 'We got our asp!'" Herman shivered—feeling some horror: "I was touched by human hands! Yecch! Yecch! And they emptied out a pickle jar and put me inside."

"Poor reptile soul!"

Herman lifted his head and let it drift. It was like a philosopher's thought, just drifting back and forth. "Imagine: a pickle jar—my prison. The fate that can overtake us!"

Now up to now I had had my reservations—if not any really severe misgivings—about snakes, lizards, worms: the creepies and crawlies. But Herman G. S.—he changed all that. I could tell he was a philosopher, albeit a timid one.

"And in this foul-smelling pickle jar they carried me back to New York. And then put me in this wicker prison."

"Don't worry, Herman." I stood up and shook. This helpless, imprisoned garter snake had brought out the savior, the impulse to save, that lurks in all dogs. "I'll help you!" Mighty I rose on my hind legs! . . .

"*How?*"

I walked my legs under me and sat down again. "I don't know yet," I was forced to admit. "But the terrors of the world I will perform! I honestly will! If I find out how. At least I'll try." At the very least I could be sincere. And hopeful too. Hope always helps. And sometimes it helps when it isn't even there. And so does being together with someone. If you're in an awful predicament, sharing the awfulness makes it less. "I'm here against my will myself. And chained to a pipe, as you can see."

"But what are they going to make me do?"

"I don't know, Herman. This *Antony and Cleopatra*—it really is a crazy play! Just hang in there, serpent!"

"I'm not a serpent! That sounds just awful. That is, I know I'm a serpent—in the museums. But I'm really just a garter snake." And snakes can't cry—but their eyes can change. They can blur. "And I want to go home! Say, listen!" His beady eyes brightened. "I know a New Jersey license plate—and if you could get me outta here, I could squiggle around—and maybe find a New Jersey car—and wrap myself around the hubcap—"

"There must be a better way," I said.

"Then think of it! *Please!*"

"I will. I promise. You just relax."

"This wicker itches."

So now I had another problem. Along with *Antony and Cleopatra*—just learning where to go, on stage, in the show—and also along with my stage fright, which got bigger as opening night got nearer—I now had Herman Garter Snake. And how to get the poor soul home. The one thing I liked about all this mess was that I got to know all different creatures—like snakes and actors.

But Herman really worried me. So lost in the city. However, if one is a genuine worrier—you never can get enough!

Dress rehearsal—for actors—is the last run-through with costumes. Dress rehearsal—for animals, at least for *this* one—is the very last chance to escape. Our dress rehearsal for *Antony and Cleopatra* occurred on a Sunday afternoon. I remember, because I had to play sick. The professor wanted to go for a walk, but I lay down and sighed and looked as bleary-eyed as I could. After feeling my nose—and I managed to sneeze—to see if I had a cold, he decided I really *was* unwell, and went out by himself. Just as soon as he'd gone, Cleopatra's cat, who'd been hiding outside, said, "Psst! Come on! We're already late." *Better never than late:* From now on that's going to be my motto, after all that happened that afternoon.

It was the first time the actors got to wear their costumes, and everybody was very excited. I thought that I'd just be wearing my fur, but as usual, I was wrong. They had this wicked-looking collar for me. Most Romans were soldiers, and since I was supposed to be a Roman dog, they decided that I should be militaristic too. The collar was made of steel, and very heavy, and had big, ugly spikes sticking out all over. The irony of a cocker spaniel who's always been a pacifist wearing this really warlike collar escaped everybody except myself.

Irma had to wear a collar too. She was hoping for an elaborate Egyptian headdress, but either because Vic thought she couldn't balance it—but she could!—or, more likely, because they couldn't afford it, she had to settle for something that Choo-Choo Melons whipped up. Although the only jewelry I've seen up close belongs to the missis—and she has little, being a teacher's wife—I believe Irma's collar was supposed to be made of rubies, emeralds, and gold. Actually, it was pieces of colored glass glued to a strip of leather that looked—and smelled—like a slice of old, overcooked steak. But still, from a distance it did look rather pretty. And one thing I've learned, from this whole appalling experience: the imagination of actors—which can turn colored glass into jewels—is a really wonderful attribute. Perhaps their best. Perhaps their only!

So all of us were psyched up to rehearse. And I was *spiked* up. Forgive that, if you can. But not Herman. He had to stay in his wicker cage. Nobody—and least of all Rita—was anxious to run through his scene. Mike Canary was backstage too, chirping and chortling at "what fools these mortals be!" By "mortals" The Bard had meant human beings, but Mike Canary meant dogs and cats too!

To save time and not change the stage settings, we didn't rehearse the scenes in order. And it so happened, by very bad luck, the first scene we did was one between Antony and that sleazy Octavius—the one who got to be emperor when everybody else got knocked off. But since Antony was in the scene, so was I. I was just supposed to follow him, and growl when he was angry and whine when he was sad and bark when he felt

like the King of the World. In other words, just echo in dog talk
everything he was feeling, you see.

"Oh, Irmy—I'm nervous!" I said, backstage.

"I've *demanded* that you not call me—"

"But I'm so scared! It's even worse than the Dogcatcher! If I
feel like this, just in dress rehearsal—whiskers!—what will
opening night be like?"

"It'll be fine, furry-face! You'll be a star! Now go out there and
knock 'em dead! Your best shot, puppy dog!"

"My best shot—right! Okay, kittycat—here I go!"

I tried to trot after Antony, as he made his entrance,
accompanied by a toot on a horn. Felipe, as well as playing
basketball, was in a band uptown. But that [swearword] collar
did me in! It weighed a ton, and I had to follow Antony down a
flight of stairs. Well, my head was dragging, and I missed the
first step, and—yes, that's right—fell down all the rest!

A ripple of giggles went through the theater. But—my best
shot, I'd promised—I picked myself up and decided to do
something very dramatic. And make them all know that *I* was
no fool!

I picked myself up—and my jaw really hurt, because I'd fallen
on my face—and looked around for Antony. There were
togas—that's what Romans wore: kind of funny-looking
dresses, for men—all over the place. And also, if you've seen one
Roman, you've seen them all! But at last I spotted Antony—I
thought I had—and to make my really dramatic gesture, I
jumped in his lap! And licked his face, to boot.

And laughter—ridicule!—burst all around me.

I was snuggling up to Octavius! Antony's dog, spiky collar
and all, in the lap of the bad guy, Antony's worst enemy!

Now, everyone gets humiliated—sooner or later. And a few
poor sensitive souls get shamed. But no one gets downright
degraded, the way I do! It must be vibrations that I put out. Or
else my whiskers. I don't know! And no one has ever gotten
derided as nastily as I was that day. The cast was in stitches.
From backstage I could hear Mikey squeaking and Irma doing
a cat guffaw.

I leaped out of Octavius's lap and ran backstage. Straight up to Irma. "Don't *ever* dare to laugh at me!"

"Why not? You're funny." She still was purring. "It was only an accident."

"You *know* I hated to be in this play!"

"Take it easy—"

"No! I won't take it easy! You always make me miserable. You *know* you make me miserable! Irma—*why* do you make me miserable?"

"Why, sweetie, so I can comfort you."

With her cat's smooth purr and her cat's smooth fur, I knew she was only joshing. But yet—but yet—there was just enough truth in what she said to drive my guts wild! "Take it off!" I screamed, and clawed my collar. "I won't be in this play!"

"Calm down!"

"I won't! Will *not!* I won't be in this play—with your ticky-tacky ludicrous friends. *They're* the fools! And so, Ms. Cat, are *you!*"

Mike Canary marched toward me. Now, ordinary birds are fluff. But Mike, with his wings held tight to his side, in a way I still don't understand, can suggest clenched fists. "Oima *wants* youz in dis play!"

"No, Mike." Irma's voice was soft, as if far off, and sad and strange. "If he wants to go—"

"Are youz two gonna fight again?" Perhaps we should have. Just bitten and scratched one another, until all the bitterness went away . . . Oh, the pettiness, the littleness of arguments— and the bigness of little things!

"No," said Irma, in that same voice: a stranger's voice, which suddenly chilled me. "We're not going to fight." Or else, in some way, she made *me* the stranger. "Not now. If Jerry wants to go—"

"I *do!*"

With her delicate claws she unfastened my collar. "Then go," she murmured.

The actors had gathered around us by now. Vic said to Rita, "We can't have any neurotic dog lousing up the production."

"Don't worry," said Rita. "The cat's everything. She'll be the whole show. Without or with Fido."

"Then go," echoed Irma—I mean, echoed herself. "You're free," she pronounced, like a judgment on me.

"Well, I will!" I snorted. "I most certainly will."

And in high dudgeon—the *highest* dudgeon!—I left. After wishing them all—my most furious *"Woof"*—*"Good luck!"*

But on the way home, as my injured pride tried to heal itself, the only thing I saw were eyes. Irma's eyes—with a strange expression fixed in them. I could not fathom it. Her eyes seemed angry . . . hurt . . . disappointed. Whatever emotions they reflected, however, they shone like true, but impassive, jewels above the phoney stones in her collar.

SEVENTEEN

Antony and Cleopatra and Irma and Me

That night I decided to run away—the most drastic decision a dog can take. But there's only so much anxiety that a cocker can stand. I leave heroism to German shepherds and Labrador retrievers. All I knew was: I had to get away. I'd had too much of New York, too many adventures, too much excitement—I was shedding, in fact. Rather badly too.

When dark came, I pawed the lock open and crept through the window. I waited till very late, however, because I was secretly hoping that Irma or Mike or *somebody* would come and tell me that everything would be all right. No one came.

But where was there to run away to? I didn't have a single idea. So I decided to walk, not run. And I walked west, towards the Hudson River. In all the weeks I'd been in New York, I had never seen the Great River up close. It looked very pretty, viewed from Mike's old lady's apartment, but more like a picture, seen through the window frame.

Bagless and hopeless, I trudged down ugly, deserted streets. The buildings looked like dinosaurs. They all had died—run-down warehouses, abandoned tenements—and now were extinct. So was I. Yet still—they retained the poetry of ruin. I did not.

And then—there it was! The Great Hudson River . . .

I walked right up to the concrete embankment. And—my word!—it truly was beautiful. They say the river's polluted now, and dogs and men can't swim in it, but Lord—oh, Lord!— is it beautiful! It flowed beneath the October night. And the night was clear. The stars were as bright and sharp as needles, but the prickles they gave me were wonderful. And a new moon too. It hung up there like the edge of a little silver fingernail, or a sly silver grin, in the sky.

I walked my legs under me and just sat down. You could jump, a part of me said to me. Of course, cockers can swim, but if I didn't dog-paddle, I'd sink. And besides, if the Hudson is *that* polluted, sink or swim, you rot anyway. What a way to go! But then, looking up—the stars; looking out—the lights, like fireflies, of New Jersey; and looking back—the enchanted skyline of New York City—I decided, "No! No jumping for me."

But still I had to do *something!* . . . The pressure of life—my dog's life—was so heavy, just then. . . .

To cry, or not to cry . . . To whimper, perhaps.

And then I had it. And then I did it.

To howl, or not to howl. That's been the story of my life. And I'd always suppressed it. I didn't now. The moon did it, I think. No dog can resist a moon.

I just *howled!* Once. "*Ah-ooooh!*" . . . And one good howl is all it takes.

And in fact it was all it took to wake up the neighbors. In a very big building nearby—Westbeth, it's called—and artists live there. The lights went on all over the place.

One howl. And suddenly I was quickly aware what I had to do. A deep decision is taken someplace, way inside you. Then it bursts the surface. And when orders come from down below, you can only obey. I recommend howling to everyone! It clears the mind—the nostrils too—and helps the heart—and stops your coat from shedding.

* * *

If it was my fate to be absurd, ridiculous—well then, I accepted it. And came into my own life, on the very next day. For Monday night, a half an hour before curtain time—the premiere performance of *Antony and Cleopatra*—I showed up at the Globetown Playhouse.

"Well look who's here," said Mike Canary, as casual as you please. He might just as well have been awaiting the garbage man. "Da second retoin a da cockerel! He keeps comin' back."

I feared to meet those gemlike and precious eyes of Irma's. But she only quizzed me silently—two opals that had sight hidden somewhere inside them—and then accepted everything. "We're both in the first scene," she reminded me.

"I know."

Then Vic and Rita noticed yours truly. They both were in costume, and hers, like all the Egyptian ladies' clothes, was very scanty. I took one look, and then glanced away. "The pooch is back," she coarsely observed.

"But can we trust him?" Vic wondered.

"*Woof!*" I said. Dog talk for "*Yes!*"

"I'm not so sure we can trust him." Vic studied me, and I gave him my most trustworthy look. "If he flubs up again, he could wreck the show. Do you think we can depend on him?"

"Mee-*ow!*" screeched Irma.

"That's a yes," said Rita, "if I ever heard a yes!"

"I'll get his collar."

They fastened that thing around my neck. And believe me— it hadn't gotten any lighter! But I resolved that my neck would break before I would ever lower my head.

"Ten minutes!" Felipe Luciano called.

"I'll be right back!"

"Irma Cat," I barked, "you stay right here! I returned only because of you!"

"I'll be right *back!*" In a flash of fur she disappeared out into the alley.

"Oh, Mike—"

"Take it easy, bud. When Oima does somet'in'—it isn't time wasted."

And he was right. For just before curtain time, Cleopatra's cat came back.

"Where *were* you? I couldn't have gone on!"

"Take a peep through the curtain."

I did. And there, confused but curious, were Big John and Big Frieda, and—well, I'll say it—*Big* Professor T and *Big* Missis! I understand now why everyone in New York is called "Big." It's this City: the size of it. Its Bigness enlarges everyone. And *my* biggies were there!

"But *how* did you get them?"

"I screamed. And I bit. The professor and his missis chased me, but when they saw our picture—"

"What picture?"

"During rehearsals a picture was taken. The human cast thought it was of them. But I made sure you and I were up front. It's posted right outside the theater."

"But Irma—"

"So I bit the professor—which seems to be a habit of mine—and he and your missis gave chase—and then on to Big Frieda's, where she and John were studying Egyptology—"

"Were they *really?*" I was so pleased.

"No, they were not. But they came anyway. And there they are."

"But Irma—" I had sudden qualms. "My *family!* I can't act in front of them!"

"Yes, you can," said the cat. "And you must. And you *will!* It is very high time that both of them know you are more than a pet."

"One minute!" Felipe called. "The houselights are going down."

"Oh! *Oh*—"

And the show—despite my severe misgivings—was on.

The first scene of *Antony and Cleopatra* takes place in Egypt. And everybody is having a party, on a terrace overlooking the river Nile. In our production there was one palm tree—and it did noble service!—which stood for Egypt. Whenever that cardboard palm tree appeared, you knew right away that you were in Egypt, and the Nile and the pyramids were just out of sight.

The first scene, like most of the scenes in the play, was mostly Antony and Cleopatra telling each other how much they were really and truly in love. I would have thought that time would suffice—just being together—if either of them had really believed it.

"If it be love indeed, tell me how much!"

That's what Cleopatra (Rita) said, as she sashayed on stage. And Irma sashayed right behind her. But with more grace, I thought. More elegance. She seemed more queenly, if you know what I mean.

Of course Cleopatra just wanted a compliment, but Antony didn't give her one. The whole thing about this play was, Antony and Cleopatra couldn't decide if they loved one another enough—and that would do—or whether they wanted to be the Egyptian Queen and the Roman King of the whole wide world.

"If it be love indeed, tell me how much!"

Well, Antony just darn wouldn't tell her, and I decided to scratch my ear. When a woman—or a queen, or a cat—acts silly, and begs you for a compliment, it's best to do something ordinary. Besides, my ear did itch.

But—my word!—the response I got! The audience loved it! I used my left hind leg and scratched!—so *there*, Cleopatra— and the audience roared. As long as I was out there, I thought, and likely to make a fool of myself, I might as well improvise. Most actors do it anyway—especially when they forget their lines. So I scratched. And the audience—wow!—it belonged to me! I had them in my paws. Even Irma shot me a glance of wonder—yes, wonder, and surprise, and pride—at the big response I drew from that little audience. The whole theater could only hold two hundred.

And laughter! And applause! I even could hear the Thompsons laughing—and that acted on me like top round ground! . . . Oh, did it ever act on me. It went straight to my head. It went also to my stubby tail. I couldn't keep myself from wagging. But I'm so short, down there, I think that only the first two rows could see.

After that first scene—during which Irma purred suggestively—we two knew that we owned that play. The spectators were in love with us. And you know something strange? The actors didn't seem to care. And actors, I have found, are not exactly the most modest of mortals. But they wanted this production of theirs to be such a smash hit—so they all could give up acting on stage and become movie stars—that they let me and Irma do anything. Because they could see that we were the smashingest hits of all. Actors ordinarily hate being upstaged, but after Scene One they even began to play their parts so that Irma and I could take over.

Then something even more wonderful happened. I mean, even stranger than Irma and I being stars of a play or me losing my stage fright. I started to *listen*—yes, listen to all those shimmering words that The Bard had given his characters to say. And he—even *me*—who begins to hear great poetry gets beautifully entrapped. He believes. Indeed, he begins to love.

It all happened towards the end of Act One. Antony decides to go to Rome and be King of the World—the dope: he should have stayed in Egypt and kept being happy—and he and Cleopatra have to say good-bye. Well, you know, I just thought they'd say, "Bye"—"Bye"—and let it go at that. But on the contrary! The queen has this really wonderful speech—in which she forgets what she's going to say! Anybody but The Bard would have just had her say, "Oh shucks! It slipped my mind!" But Shakespeare's Cleopatra is so much in love—and so really, soulfully, Big—that she says, "Oh! My oblivion is very Antony, and I am all forgotten." . . . Isn't that *fabulous*?

Then later, in Act Two, there came some even greater lines. Our Antony has a sidekick whose name is Enobarbus, and he is describing to a bunch of everybody how Cleopatra looked the first time her Antony saw her. She was on a ship, and she wanted to make a *big* impression! So Shakespeare says, "The barge she sat in, like a burnished throne, burned on the water—"

When I heard those words, two revelations hit my head. The first was—Beauty! It was then I knew what Professor T doesn't. Poetry—whatever it is—is made up of all those words that make the whole world seem more real! And that description will have to do. And indeed it *does* do, very well!

My second revelation was—Irma! Now, Shakespeare's been dead for ages, of course, but it just suddenly hit my brain that in the character of Cleopatra The Bard had been describing My Cat. I've never seen Irma on a barge of gold—but I've seen her sitting on top of the clothes dryer. And she certainly looks like a queen up there!

And a few minutes later that Barbus guy said something even more to the point. Describing Cleopatra, he said, "Age cannot wither her, nor custom stale her infinite variety." Translated to dog talk, that means the queen was aging well and she still had a few surprises left. But *my* thought was—*It's Irmy! It's Irma again!* Translated into Irma's own life—"Age cannot wither her"—that means, for a cat, she doesn't look a day over five; "Nor custom stale her infinite variety"—and whiskers knows what she'll do next!

My presence was not required during this scene, and sitting backstage, I was so absorbed I didn't notice Herself approach. "What's up, puppy dog? You look mesmerized."

"Shhh! Please! Just listen, Irma. Those words—they are so beautiful! I didn't know *words* could be so passionate and fine."

"Mm!" purred the cat. "The Bard will be so pleased you approve."

"Oh, don't make fun! I love this, Irma—"

Indeed—oh, indeed I did. . . .

And by Act Three I was living that play more completely—and even enjoying it more, I guess—than I was living and enjoying my life. Life always seems to be coming later. But not that night. It was *now!*

* * *

But Acts Three and Four kind of slipped by yours truly unnoticed. It may have been they were just too confusing—and I'd say that to The Bard's face himself. That idiot Antony married the sister of weasel Octavius, by way of becoming King of the World. But it didn't quite work out that way. Cleopatra, nat'rally, was furious. She almost tore the Egyptian throne to shreds. And Irma helped. But then Antony and the Queen were reunited, and then they had *another* fight, about that naval battle. But thinking about it afterwards, I realized that there had to be sadness, and anger, and unhappiness, for there to be glory. What else is tragedy all about? (Or Life?)

But it wasn't really the plot that confused me. The plot—I mean, Antony and Cleopatra—it all is part of real history. But then, real history too is a mess. And it doesn't happen in such lovely words. It's that—I had made up my mind to say something. I meant—ye gods!—to declare myself.

At the very first opportunity, when Irma and I were alone backstage, I nudged her into a corner and said, "Irma Cat, just sit on your barge—or that crate over there—I have something to say!"

"You got a problem, puppy dog? Just go out in the alley—"

"I have no problem!" But ah, I did! "I have something to say." Because speaking your feelings is difficult. "I just want you to know—I mean, what I feel is—oh, whiskers, Irma, *I love you a lot!* So there!"

Her eyes—those yellow opals—narrowed and stared. "You love me?"

"Yes I do! And if it be love indeed—then Irmy, I want to tell you how much."

"*Mhmm!*" she purred, somewhat skeptically.

But I had to be honest. "I'm sure I do love you, Irma Cat. But on the other paw, perhaps I am just being swept away by the glory of the poetry."

"I thought I detected a Shakespearean lilt—"

"No! [Swearword!] I mean it!" The truth burst out. The truth always bursts out. That's one of the ways that you know it's true. "I do love you, Irma! These weeks we've been through thick and thin, good times and bad, for better or worse, and—

and—" My heart collapsed, from just the way she was looking at me. "And—I love you, Irma Cat. Whether you're a dusty Graymalkin, or Mikey Canary's friend—or even—alas!—the pet of a cop—I love you, Irma Cat! I do! And now—if *you* would like to say something—"

She had nothing to say. At first. But then—as her eyes widened bright—even brighter than footlights—she said, "Where *did* you come from, Jerry, my lad? I cannot even imagine where! But wherever it was, my dearest dog, I'm very glad that you're here."

She hadn't said that she loved me, of course. But her tail brushed my lips; she batted my nose with a paw—and then kissed me where she had batted it. It wasn't much. But from some people—and Irma is one—not-much is enough.

"Come on," she said. "We've got our death scenes now. This is it, babe. Now we knock 'em dead!"

Our Antony's death, as I've said, was a bust. He fell on his sword, and missed. Whether Ol' Vic thought that *I* might die by falling on a sharp Milk Bone—oh well, it was a tragedy. So they dragged him off to some marble hideout where Cleopatra was holed up.

And there he said, "I am dying, Egypt—dying." Which would be rather like my saying to Irma, "I am dying, Greenwich Village—dying!"

But he really did die in earnest then, in Cleopatra's arms, and I tried to do my dramatic thing: *howl*—in abject sorrow—tragically!

But howling, moonwise, beside the Hudson, is not like howling in a cramped little theater. I really meant to shoot the works—*"Ahhhh!"*—and bring tears to the eyes of the audience—but something—life!—got stuck in my throat, and I shrieked, in a high falsetto, *"Eeeeee!"*

To be embarrassed is simply my fate. I turned my head on Vic's big chest. But he was nice. The audience was roaring with laughter, but good Ol' Vic lifted up his hand—and he was supposed to be dead, remember—and petted my head, just to

let me know that he still liked me, despite the awful shriek I'd shrieked.

I was starting to have deep loving thoughts about the goodness of *some* human beings—but suddenly, at this critical juncture, Choo-choo Melons came in with the asp.

"Can't anyone help me? Please? Anyone?" Poor Herman! They had tied him down with dental floss. Because they knew that rope would show, and any terrified snake could break string. The asp was supposed to be hidden in a basket of figs, but the actors couldn't find any figs, so they used some McIntosh apples instead.

But poor Herman! "Oooo!" he moaned. "Can't anyone help me? *Ooooo!*" And he was lifted up. That is, the wicker basket was. "*Ooooo!*" And pressed against Rita's chest. And Cleopatra died of snakebite. As a matter of fact, however, I doubt if they ever really made contact. I think that Rita was just as little attracted to Herman as he to her.

But before she died, Cleopatra had the most wonderful words in the play. In fact—in the whole wide world! She said she had "immortal longings in her." And of course Irma *always* has immortal longings in her! I was listening, lying on Antony's chest, where I was supposed to have died of despair. Or maybe I had just simply died of drama.

And then Cleopatra said, "I am Fire and Air. My other elements I give to baser life."

And I thought again—*Irma!* This play's about Irma. She's Fire and Air. And her baser elements she left on the Upper East Side, with the Nussters.

And that's about it. Modesty forbids me—or at least it encourages me—not to describe the ovation we got. A *standing* ovation, if you please!

Backstage, when the curtain had fallen—collapsed, is more like it—I saw dear Herman squiggling away, and I said—I was still in the mood—"Now whither away, O asp?"

"New Jersey, you ham actor you! And as soon as I find a New Jersey license plate!"

"I'll fly youz dere," said Mike, who had most thoroughly enjoyed the drama—onstage and off.

So Mike Canary flew Herman Garter Snake home. And Herman—bless his reptile heart!—said that he'd like to see me again. "But can this canary fly *you*—a plump cocker spaniel—"

"Please!"

"—across the River?"

"We'll take da Path tubes," said Mike.

And the last I saw, Mike had gripped Herman G. S. very firmly, but gently, in his bill and was heading west. The great direction. It leads across the continent—and its first stop is beautiful New Jersey.

Then came the final curtain calls. And modesty forbids again. I wish it didn't forbid so much!

First: human beings, nat'rally. They wouldn't take second place.

And then Irma and me! *(I!)*

We bowed. I heard the laughter and clapping of Professor and Mrs. T. I heard the hearty roaring approval of Big John—and the bravos of Frieda. There were even a few policemen there whom Big John had coerced into coming. And clapping. In short, I heard the World saying *"Yes!"* And *yes!* too can be a frightening word!

But in the very midst of this Bliss, I felt Irma nudge me and say, "Furry-face—my dear—try not to believe. Or only believe what's real. They'll be clapping for somebody else, next week."

That rather deflated me.

"And remember—if that charming head gets too large, I still can call—and I *always* can call—!"

I know. Oh, I know! . . .

I *still* am scared of the Dogcatcher!

Poor Little Cigarette—
she had no home but the streets

FLIGHT
OF THE
SPARROW

BY JULIA CUNNINGHAM

author of *Dorp Dead*

When Mago found her, she was in the furnace room
of the orphanage. He gave her a name—Little Cigarette—and brought her to his home, the streets of
Paris. For Cigarette, it was almost like having a real
family—and Mago gave her the courage to survive.

But survival sometimes means having to hurt those
you care most about. And when Cigarette is forced to
steal a valuable painting from an artist friend, she
must flee Paris. Armed only with love, she begins a
frightening and extraordinary journey to try to make
things right. Maybe she can earn a chance at happiness that Mago and the other street people never
had.

"Exciting and poignant."—School Library Journal*

AN AVON CAMELOT ● 57653-8 ● $1.95

*Meet the most rebellious, unmanageable, and lov-
able foster child of all time, in one of the funniest,
most touching and widely acclaimed books of
all time!*

Katherine Paterson

**Winner of The National Book Award
A Newbery Honor Book**

*"A finely written story. . . . Its characters linger
long in the readers thoughts after it is finished."*
The Washington Post

"Tough and touching" School Library Journal

An Avon Camelot Book   45963 • $1.75

Also by Katherine Paterson
Bridge to Terabithia   55301 • $1.95
The Sign of the Chrysanthemum   49288 • $1.75
Of Nightingales That Weep   51110 • $1.95
Angels & Other Strangers   51144 • $1.95